IRRESISTIBLE

"You do not like me."

"No," she said, "I do not believe I do."

"No," I said, "you do not like me, you *love* me! You want to *ravish* me!" I sat on the ground and patted my lap.

She gave a bark of laughter. "You are mad!" she cried and skipped away, a chuckle dancing in the air behind her.

I *was* mad—mad with a desire to kiss her! I stared after her, shaking my head.

Apple was a different person since she'd come here. I'd never seen her smile so much. She was irresistible there in the sunshine, with the wind blowing through her dark hair, her cheeks full of roses, and her eyes full of sparkling light . . .

BOOK YOUR PLACE ON OUR WEBS
AND MAKE THE
READING CONNECTION!

We've created a customized website just for our very special readers, where you can get the inside scoop on everything that's going on with Zebra, Pinnacle and Kensington books.

When you come online, you'll have the exciting opportunity to:

- View covers of upcoming books
- Read sample chapters
- Learn about our future publishing schedule (listed by publication month *and author*)
- Find out when your favorite authors will be visiting a city near you
- Search for and order backlist books from our online catalog
- Check out author bios and background information
- Send e-mail to your favorite authors
- Meet the Kensington staff online
- Join us in weekly chats with authors, readers and other guests
- Get writing guidelines
- AND MUCH MORE!

Visit our website at
http://www.kensingtonbooks.com

A
PERFECT
GEM

MELYNDA BETH SKINNER

ZEBRA BOOKS
Kensington Publishing Corp.
www.kensingtonbooks.com

ZEBRA BOOKS are published by

Kensington Publishing Corp.
850 Third Avenue
New York, NY 10022

All Kensington titles, imprints, and distributed lines are avail-
able at special quantity discounts for bulk purchases for sales
promotion, premiums, fund-raising, educational, or institu-
tional use.

Special book excerpts or customized printings can also be created to fit specific needs. For details, write or phone the
office of the Kensington Special Sales Manager: Attn. Special
Sales Department. Kensington Publishing Corp., 850 Third
Avenue, New York, NY 10022. Phone: 1-800-221-2647.

Zebra and the Z logo Reg. U.S. Pat. & TM Off.

ISBN 0-8217-7839-0

First Printing: September 2005
10 9 8 7 6 5 4 3 2 1

Printed in the United States of America

*For Mary Louise Wells,
with gratitude and love.
Yes, Penelope, you may
look inside my notebook!*

Some counterfeits reproduce so very well the truth that it would be a flaw of judgment not to be deceived by them.
—François, Duc De La Rochefoucauld

It is a bawdy planet . . .
—William Shakespeare

PROLOGUE

Somewhere in England, Last Week

"Never give a child a name like Felicity or Earnest, my dears"—the old woman shook her head—"for too often Felicity's a shrew and Earnest a liar."

A murmur of anticipation sifted through the lengthening shadows as the dozen young women scattered about the comfortable winter parlor gathered closer to the storyteller. Still handsome in her seventies, with red hair streaked gray, a straight back, and strong, expressive hands, Erma was a loving and remarkably intelligent woman, who enjoyed a bit of fun now and then.

"Have a care who you marry," she said, "because it's the same with surnames." She smiled into the fire. "That's how it was with Leah Grey."

The younger women all looked to the eight portraits on the wall. From one, a small woman with dark hair and eyes stared mischievously back. She wore pretty Jane Austen–style clothing and a soft, dancing smile.

"Leah was a responsible thing," Erma went on. "A workaholic, you might say, who ran an inn. She was dependable, forthright—a real straight arrow. *And*"—she smoothed

her hands lovingly over the arms of her chair—"she sat ri
here in this very chair, once upon a time."

The younger ladies exchanged smiles and settled in for
another exciting tale. Erma had an endless supply.

"She wasn't a shrew or a liar, of course. Oh, no! But our
Miss Leah Grey could see no shades of gray at all," she
went on. "For her, the world was painted a reassuring black
and white.

"And as for Posthumous Jones, he was. . . . Well, perhaps I should save that for the end of the story. For now,
it's enough to say that both of them had a lot to learn."
She chuckled and, tucking a soft quilt in around her,
folded her hands over her lap and settled into her chair.

"They met in 1811, in a sleepy old village tucked away
in the hills not far from here, though their story really
began many years before that." She pointed to the wide
mantle. "Would one of you hand me that box up there?"

A willowy blonde of perhaps twenty carefully took the
box down. "It looks like an antique," she said. "Is it?"

"It came with the house." Drawing a key from her pocket,
Erma turned the box's lock and lifted several slim, leather
volumes from inside before closing—and locking—the box
once more. Then she opened the first book.

"Lower Ridington, England," she read, "Eighteen-
eleven . . ."

CHAPTER ONE

Lower Ridington, England, 1811

> *The newspapers are abuzz with news that the Earl of Instep will announce the fate of a large sapphire of singular quality a fortnight hence. I am confident you are clever enough to acquire it. If you do, I can promise you will acquire knowledge of your mother's fate as well. I will find you at The Dancing Maiden. Once again the jewel bends the course of your life.*

Before pulling that blasted, blessed note from my pocket to read yet again, I was nothing but a carefully nondescript man dressed in utterly nondescript clothing, as I always was in that tiny village. But when I unfolded the thing that time, the soft-worn folds of the foolscap ripped, and I swore—eloquently, judging by the startled stares of those seated nearby.

"Beg pardon, ma'am," I murmured politely to one lady, stuffing the note back into my pocket. I was genuinely contrite, too, until she looked me from head to toe, curled her lip with haughty disdain, and pinched up her face as though she'd suddenly had a pineapple stuffed down her expensive corset.

Then something snapped inside, and instead of
siding as I ought, I doffed my cap instead and winked
her. "Cold outside," I said, "but I wager *you* are nice an
warm." It was a blatant proposition, as rude as they came,
and when her eyes bugged and she turned her back with
a *harumph*, I laughed loudly and quaffed my ale.

So much for blending in.

It was almost forgivable. I was short on patience. For
three hours I'd waited with no result. Clearly, whoever had
written the unsigned note would approach only after I had
stolen the gem.

Sitting at my usual table at The Dancing Maiden, I spun
a little medallion of mine—a good luck charm of sorts,
though it hadn't brought me what I most sought—on the
oaken tabletop in apparent idleness, but I was really
scanning the crowd the while. In spite of the largish
quantity of ale I'd downed, my nerves were pulled as
tight as bowstrings. I was on the lookout for anyone out
of the ordinary. A single, stolen glance might give away
the note's composer, but the seconds marched relentlessly
by and still nothing.

The weather was terrible that night, and the howling
wind found its way inside the inn, sending the lamp-lit
shadows dancing across the walls. I sighed. As the hours
crept by, my own shadows were the only things that
seemed to mark my presence. There wasn't a person
there I thought could have written the note.

What had I expected? A blasted miracle?

I quaffed another hefty draught of The Maiden's fine
ale. Why not expect a miracle? I had given up any hope
of finding my mother, or even of learning where her
bones lay, years ago. The note in my pocket was miracle
enough. Why not ask for two?

Because, my heart said, *you do not deserve either.*

Swearing under my breath, I finished off the ale and
slammed the tankard down with a little too much force,
eliciting a frown from the proprietress. She was a winsome

little thing, slightly plump with dark curls and laughing
eyes as dark as a night sea.

She glared at me from behind the bar, and I gave a
deliberately provocative smile, tapped the rim of my
tankard, and crooked my finger at her, winking. She
picked up a pitcher and approached.

"More?" she asked, lifting the pitcher a little.

"How can you offer a man more when you haven't
even given him the first taste?" I patted my lap for perhaps the thousandth time.

It was a game between us, repeated over and over in the
eight years I'd been coming to The Dancing Maiden. Normally, dimples magically appeared in her smooth cheeks
as she rolled her eyes, turned her back, and walked heart-
lessly away. Tonight however, she smiled tightly, licked her
lips, and flicked her gaze nervously to where my hands
rested atop my breeches.

She was tempted!

And I was stunned.

Erma chuckled and, opening a second volume without
closing the first, continued reading.

For a moment, I actually considered it. I had been
waiting for most of an hour for an opportunity to move
closer to him without actually appearing as though I
wanted to move closer—which was difficult, as he seemed
even more watchful than usual—but sitting on his lap was
not what I had in mind. That was a little too close.

I understate the matter. It was devilishly close. Foolishly
close. Disastrously close.

After a moment's hesitation, I shook my head and
tisked. "You are a rogue."

"You have no idea," he said.

Oh, yes, I do! I thought, moving away, for I had learned

something about him, something I was sure he didn't want anyone to know: he wasn't what he seemed!

His name was Jack Morgan, and he was a frequent though irregular customer of ours. He always sat at the same table, the small round one in the corner nearest our wide front door. That table was scarred and wobbly, but from it he commanded an excellent view of the common room.

Of medium height and build, he had curly, dark hair worn neither short nor long, and large, strong-looking hands neither rough nor smooth. His clothing was of average quality, neither in the latest style nor so old that they marked him as a man who couldn't afford new clothes, and the colors he wore were always nondescript earthen hues that did not draw the eye. There was nothing exceptional about him at first glance.

But if one looked closer, one began to see Mr. Morgan was different. Very different.

He never truly relaxed, for one thing. He always sat with a calm, even indolent ease, but his blue eyes missed nothing, and I sensed he could spring at a moment's notice. He often worried a coin in his hand or spun it atop his table, and he seemed always to be watching people—including me.

Of course, since The Dancing Maiden was mine, I was there all of the time, and though we'd never had any deep conversations, we had traded quips and often shared a conspiratorial smile at the antics of those around us. Those moments made me feel as though I knew him, though that was but a fancy; he shared little of himself. Still, I liked what he had allowed me to see.

He never drank to excess, though he quaffed more ale than most men. He was quiet. Obviously intelligent. Unfailingly polite. He always praised my food with, "Mmm . . . delicious, miss. Thank you," in a soft, rich-toned voice sounding more like a caress than a compliment. And even when trying to tempt me to his lap, he used proper diction and grammar—a puzzlement, that. The refined voice suggested gentry, while his coarse clothing and frank manner pointed to a rung considerably lower on the social ladder. A workingman of some sort, though his hands were deft and not so rough. Perhaps a merchant or a clerk, I'd decided, but no higher.

If ever I'd climbed onto his oft-proffered lap, I might have learnt the truth before it was too late!

I chanced another glance into his corner. He was watching me! Smiling roguishly, he patted his thigh again. This time I remembered my wits and rolled my eyes as I should have the first time. He issued the same amused invitation every time I came near his table, chuckling softly when I refused. I'd been offended at first, years ago, but it had become a game after a while, and I'd come to look forward to the lunge and parry of it.

Until tonight. Until I'd discovered what Uncle John had pilfered from Mr. Morgan's suspiciously tattered pocket. Uncle, you see, had a habit of *borrowing* things.

I bustled about the common room of my little inn trying to look busier than I actually was, the "trinket" Uncle had borrowed burning a hole in my apron pocket and Mr. Morgan's eyes boring a hole between my shoulder blades. I had to find a way to return Uncle's trophy to Mr. Morgan unnoticed, yet sitting on that rogue's lap was out of the question. Curse the man! His eyes were too alert. I could neither get close enough to slip the thing into his coat pocket unnoticed nor leave it lying about and pretend it had been there all the time. He would know I was lying immediately.

For, whereas battered snuffboxes or tarnished farthings might go unheeded on the floor, huge perfect gems worth a king's ransom tend to attract notice!

CHAPTER TWO

The excessive increase of anything often causes a reaction in the opposite direction.

—Plato

I still remember the first time Uncle presented me with one of his finds. It was a few weeks after I'd inherited The Dancing Maiden. Depositing a handkerchief next to the dry sink behind the bar, he'd looked for all the world like Puss dropping one of her grisly offerings at my feet.

"There!" he'd said, proudly. "Look at that!"

I picked up the delicate handkerchief and examined the intricate initials embroidered on it. "S-E-F," I said, scanning the common room and wondering which of the guests had dropped it.

The Maiden was crowded that evening, but it wasn't difficult to spot SEF. She was the only woman in the room not wearing sensible, serviceable clothing. Perched on a chair as though she might fall ill if she touched too much of it, the silly chit wore a frothy creation of white muslin sprigged with tiny, yellow primroses the same color as the initials of her snowy handkerchief.

"What a gem!" I said under my breath.

"A diamond of the first water," Uncle said.

"A diamond of the silliest water, more like." I tried not to stare at her perfect blonde curls, so unlike my own dark, unruly hair. She wore hers short and smartly coiffed. I wore mine pulled into a serviceable bunch at the nape of my neck. Suddenly, the new red ribbon I wore seemed pretentious, a pathetic attempt at mimicking my betters, though I'd thought it rather jaunty an hour before.

I tried to tear my gaze away from the other girl's perfect figure, perfect gown, perfect skin, perfect *everything*, failing miserably. I couldn't look away. In those days, I was still young enough to be envious of the young ladies who occasionally passed through Lower Ridington on their way to London for their seasons.

"She's going to get that silly gown of hers dirty," I'd told Uncle John.

"She has a maid," he offered.

"She also has feathers for brains," I shot back, *sotto voce*, starting toward Miss Featherbrain's table. Reaching her privileged, spoiled, rich, self-righteous side, I held out the handkerchief. "Is this yours, miss?"

"Oh! How odd," she said, reaching for her reticule. The little bag's top was tightly closed with its yellow silk drawstrings. "How did I drop that? I am certain it was in my reticule when we—"

"Obviously, Caroline, you are wrong," her chaperone snapped. "Again," she added for good measure. "Really, you must take better care of your things. I shall have to report this lapse to your mama and papa. Handkerchiefs do not grow on trees." She glared at me and took the handkerchief. "The servingmaid will want a gratuity," the dragon told her charge as though I wasn't there, "and you shall pay her, to teach you a lesson."

Pulling myself up to my full height—which, at fifteen years of age, wasn't any more impressive than it is now, alas—I raised a deliberately ironical eyebrow. "I am *the proprietress* of The Dancing Maiden, madam." It wasn't a lie, not exactly. Since my parents' death, the inn had really belonged to my uncle, but Madam Pinched-Up didn't have to know that. Besides, I was the one who ran the place. Uncle didn't know the first thing about running The Maiden and never had. I raised my chin, the better to look down upon Madam Pinched-Up. "It is my duty and my pleasure to return lost articles to my guests. Neither money nor thanks are expected—or wanted."

The woman grunted and turned back to stirring her tea, which was clearly more important than I was.

But I was surprised to discover her charge had more manners. *Thank you!* the girl mouthed with a timid glance at the dragon.

I smiled, gave a nod, changed her name from Miss Featherbrains to Princess Primrose, and turned back to the bar, suddenly glad I was who I was and not some pampered, pedigreed, and imprisoned jewel of the *ton*. I might be an orphan who worked all day and half the night, but at least I was independent of action and thought, while girls such as Primrose had no freedom, and if they dared harbor independent thoughts, they certainly wouldn't be allowed to express them openly. Yes, I was happy. I lived in a world filled with the steady rhythm of honest work. Rain or shine, customers or none, hungry or full, day or night. The future was all reassuringly predictable.

Or so I thought.

Unfortunately, after that night, Uncle's new habit picked up speed. He was already a peculiar old man, set in his ways, and nothing I could say or do would persuade him to give up borrowing things from our unsuspecting guests. So I did the only thing I could. I learned to return the items—surreptitiously, if I could, and openly in the rare circumstance where I could not: "Excuse me, sir, but is that your snuffbox there on the floor near the door?"

Behind the bar, in a special cupboard, we kept a diagram of the common room. Every table and chair was represented, and we took care never to disturb the actual arrangement. When Uncle borrowed something, he would promptly place it in the cupboard upon the appropriate spot on our diagram so that I would know to whom it belonged.

I didn't like it, but Uncle was odd and elderly, and there was little I could do about it, so I dealt with it as best I could.

But now Uncle had borrowed something from Mr. Morgan.

How Uncle managed to take the sapphire in the first place I did not know. He'd never been able to borrow anything from the alert Mr. Morgan before. Yet here was the jewel in my apron pocket, pulsing to the beat of my own nervous heart and proving that Mr. Morgan was more than he seemed. *More than he wanted to seem.*

He was neither a farmer nor a run-of-the-mill merchant. Farmers and merchants did not carelessly traipse about the country with jewels the size of the Blarney Stone in their pockets. Botheration, even minor lords did not possess such things, and if they did, they treated them with more care than Mr. Morgan had thus far. No, my "Mr. Morgan" was beyond wealthy. He was deuced, devilish wealthy, an obscenely rich merchant. Perhaps even a peer!

Which meant I was in real danger.

Were I caught with his sapphire in my hand, he might think I stole it. In the mind of a judge, wealth would compensate for any unfortunate lack of family connection, while a peerage would be enough to convict me without a hearing. If I couldn't find a way to return the gem unnoticed, things could go very badly indeed. I could be transported—or worse.

Still, I was not truly worried. I had returned hundreds of Uncle's pilfered trophies over the years. I was very good at slipping a coin into a pocket here, a glove under a hat there. And though I was a little nervous, I did not doubt that in a few moments I would set things to right.

The Maiden occupied a prime spot at the top of a
shady knoll on the busy North Road. Business was always
good, and I normally employed several servingmaids,
but a cold drizzle had been falling since dawn, filling the
Maiden to its blackened rafters and creating a plausible
excuse for my needing to serve. Hefting a tray heavy
with tankards, I made my way through the crowd toward
Mr. Morgan's table, feigning a stumble as I passed, and
let spill the tray. As I'd planned, Mr. Morgan, along with
several other guests, bolted to their feet to avoid a shower
of ale, jostling and bumping each other, whilst I deftly
slipped my left hand into my apron and—

And then, as it always does when disaster strikes, time
seemed to slow down.

My fingers curled around the sapphire. I remember its
warmth, can still feel the wide planes of its intricate
facets. Cradling it in my palm, I drew it forth and slipped
it back . . . into . . . his . . . coat—

Just as I let go of the jewel, a strong hand locked onto
my wrist. The jewel had dropped to the floor of his
pocket, but—dear heaven!—my whole blasted hand was
in his pocket as well!

"Looking for something, Apple?" he drawled.

Apple was a pet name he'd called me since the day he'd
first walked into the inn, when I'd blushed profusely at
his outrageous flirtation. But this time, there was no mischievous smile to go with it. Instead, the smile that always
made me happy inside had been replaced with a mere
mask of amusement, a smile that didn't reach his blue
eyes. A hard smile that glinted and made my heart fall.

"I haven't seen you blush like that in years," he said.

I pasted on a fake smile and said, "Would you not blush
if someone caught you apparently picking his pocket?"

"Apparently?"

I put my other hand on my hip. "What, do you think
I *meant* to put my hand in your pocket?" I laughed. "How
absurd! It is warm in here, especially when one is work-

ing. I was faint and lost my balance, and—pray, why are you shaking your head?"—

"Denials aren't working. Best to jibe and sail in the other direction."

I closed my mouth and did exactly as he suggested. "Ah. I see. You think I am a-a thief! A pickpocket!"

His eyes darted to the other guests, who were staring at us with slack-jawed speculation. Breaking into an easy laugh that suggested he thought I was jesting, he let go of my hand and motioned to the chair next to him. "Sit and have a drink with me, Miss Grey."

It was a command, not a request, and I knew it, but the rest of my guests didn't. They turned away and went back to the more interesting business of drinking and telling tales, flirting and gossiping. They hadn't noticed he'd called me "Miss Grey" instead of "Apple," as he always did.

"Thank you, but I must clean up this mull," I said, bending to pick up the tray.

"'Ere, now!" Anne, one of my servingmaids said. "I'll get that, miss. Are you 'urt?"

I shook my head.

"Nonsense. Miss Grey is yet faint," said Mr. Morgan. "She needs to sit." He pulled out the chair next to his. "*I insist.*"

Anne looked doubtfully from me to him, and I said quietly, "Perhaps I should sit for a moment. Thank you for clearing the spill, Anne."

Mr. Morgan held the chair for me, and I sat, trying to remain calm. The sapphire was back in his pocket. Mr. Morgan could prove nothing. *Uncle is safe. The Maiden's reputation is safe. All will be well.*

I took a steady breath and, raising my chin a notch, looked him in the eye.

He steepled his fingers and flicked a glance at the puddle of ale. "Thank goodness your clothing seems none the worse for the mishap," he observed, his eyes making a lazy traverse of my form from head to toe. "Hardly a drop," he said. "Almost as though you had planned it."

"Indeed," I said.

"But you did not plan it."

"No."

"I thought not." He smiled, a brittle expression, and I felt a chill in my bones. "Two mugs of Miss Grey's fine ale," he told Betsy, a second servingmaid who had hurried over to take care of the mess.

She looked to me for confirmation, and I nodded, my heart pounding in my chest. "Yes, sir." Betsy bobbed a curtsey and moved off to fetch the ale.

"They all answer to you."

I nodded. "Of course."

"Your parents bequeathed The Dancing Maiden to you."

"How do you know that?"

He ignored the question. "And you have worked hard to keep it and would hate to lose it."

"Yes . . ."

"And not just because it is their legacy to you but because it is you and your employees' entire livelihood. Not to mention the anchor for the entire village—"

"What are you getting at?" I demanded.

"—without which you and your Uncle would be begging scraps?" He sat back in his chair. "In the Colonies, perhaps?"

It was a threat, of course—one an obscenely wealthy man was quite capable of carrying out. All it would take was a motivated magistrate and the next time Uncle borrowed something—there was absolutely no way to stop Uncle from borrowing; I'd tried everything—he'd be sent to some penal colony or other. A one-way passage, at Uncle's advanced age. He would be seventy-five next birthday.

Sly on the one hand, daffy on the other, cynical one moment and tenderly sentimental the next, Uncle is an odd old dear. We loved each other greatly, we were the last of our family, and I wasn't going to lose him.

It was time to change tacks again.

"What do you want?" I asked, moistening my lips and leaning forward, ever so slightly.

Now, I am not classically beautiful. I am too plump and too dark, rather than petite and pale and blonde, but my features are not unpleasing, and my figure has been quite fine since I was twelve. I'd never had a lack of admirers, and I'd learnt quickly that a little harmless flirting with my customers was a spectacularly successful way to bring in more money. I'd become good at it, though I'd never thought I'd be using it on Mr. Morgan!

I gave a slow, demure blink and looked up at him through a veil of lashes. "I vow, sir, I will do *anything* to preserve The Maiden." He already thought I was a pickpocket; what was the harm if I convinced him I was a trollop, too?

"Anything, hmm?"

I nodded, knowing I was safe. My fanny had been pinched and patted any number of times while I worked but never by him. Except for his come-hither invitations to sit on his lap, he'd never behaved in an ungentlemanly way. So I was certain he wouldn't take me up on my implied offer, but men can be made pliable by the application of a little feminine flattery, and certain offers are the best sort of flattery. I widened my eyes, made a little *O* with my mouth, and blinked. "Anything."

He raised one speculative eyebrow.

I swallowed, suddenly alert without quite knowing why.

He laughed, stood up, and pushed in his chair.

I put my hands on my hips. "Where are you going?"

"Why, to your chamber, of course," he murmured with a roguish grin, a grin that once more reached his eyes.

Inside my chest, my heart flopped around like a fish on the sand while an abashed joy wrestled with an unbridled panic.

He sketched a deep bow and gestured broadly. "After you, my dear."

Panic won, and I . . .

. . . was delighted at her crimson blush. It spread rapidly upward from her heart, over the swell of her bosom, and to her neck, a neck I'd longed to kiss since the moment I'd seen her.

Not that I intended to take her under these circumstances. She was offering her charms only to get herself out of trouble. She wasn't serious, and I wasn't a fool.

I intended to dine at the table of Miss Grey's delights someday, but it wouldn't be a quick, quiet encounter upstairs at The Dancing Maiden. Oh, no! It would be slow, languorous—and definitely not quiet if I had anything to do with it. I'd had my eye on a wide meadow full of wildflowers a league or so outside the village, with an apple tree right in the middle and tall grass that would shield a prone couple. It was perfect. *She* was perfect.

I'd been stopping at The Dancing Maiden since I was a few days shy of twenty, a little over eight years ago, now. She'd been a delectable sixteen then, and she'd been fascinated with me. She was just too proper and too busy to admit it—even to herself, I expected. Not that I let that stop me from trying.

I knew Leah Grey's prim, demure exterior concealed a hellcat with her tail on fire. I'd seen her eyes flash with anger on the rare occasion she had to have someone ejected from the common room or when some imperious member of the *ton* deigned to stay at The Maiden and found the accommodations lacking. The hellcat always charged them triple, much to my delight. But her passions ran to laughter as easily as anger, and she often laughed until her eyes watered and her knees were weak.

She was going to taste as good as she looked—all sweet and dark and soft—but not today.

Her hands shook as she opened her chamber door. I followed her inside and, closing the door, I locked it behind me. I wasn't going to have my way with her, but that left me with another problem. She'd seen my fake sapphire. When the real one was stolen, the news would be all over the countryside. Of course, thieves' honor would demand that she not turn me in, and I thought she was honorable and would hold to that code, but I couldn't trust my own judgement. After all, I hadn't realized she was a thief until she'd almost taken the fake sapphire from my pocket! When news of the theft of the Instep Sapphire hit Lower Ridington, would there be a reward for its return? Would she identify me as the thief?

She might—unless she became my accomplice. I took a step closer.

"I am needed downstairs," she blurted.

"They will get along without you."

"They will think it odd I left."

"You were faint and dropped the tray. No one will find it odd that you needed a rest."

"But everyone saw us ascend the stairs together. And I do not want to be here," she finished with conviction.

"No one will know we both entered your chamber unless you tell them. And you came here of your own free will."

"I came here because you think I tried to steal your sapphire."

"How do you know it was a sapphire?"

"I saw it!" I saw her swallow hard. "I-I saw it on the floor. And it surprised me, and that is why I dropped the tray. I-I scooped it up, and I was returning it to your pocket before someone else could see it."

I shook my head. "Sorry, sweet, but you're as bad a liar as you are a thief."

She flinched as though I'd hit her, and her face flushed an even deeper shade of red. "I am not a thief, sir! You take that back!"

"Very well . . . we shall let the magistrate decide, then."

"No!"

I watched her flush an even deeper shade of red, and her hands began to tremble. "No, I-I told you . . . I will do anything."

I frowned, knowing suddenly that she meant it, the poor thing. It was time to put an end to her suffering. I looked across the room. "Is that your wardrobe?" I said, pointing to a tall, pine cupboard.

She narrowed her eyes. "You don't intend to lock me in, do you?"

I laughed. "My, I had no idea what a naughty girl you were. That does sound like an intriguing game. Alas, I have no time for such pleasantries. We are due at a grand house party in Yorkshire six days hence, and we must leave early on the morrow."

"We?"

I opened the cupboard. "Good God, are these all the clothes you have?"

"Do not change the subject. Did you say 'we'?"

I pulled out the best frock of the meager lot, a dark blue cotton affair that looked better suited to cleaning the stables than to attending church. "This will have to do. Wear it tomorrow. You may leave the rest here. We shall procure a new gown or two before the party."

At the mere mention of new gowns and house parties, any other woman would have peppered me with questions, but Leah Grey only scowled and crossed her arms. "Well?"

"'Well what?"

"I came here expecting to be ravished, sir. Explain yourself."

"Oh, very well." I threw my hands up in mock resignation. "If you insist upon a ravishing, I suppose I shall have to oblige, but I must warn you that we shall have to be quicker than either of us would like."

CHAPTER THREE

Seldom, very seldom, does complete truth belong to any human disclosure; seldom can it happen that something is not a little disguised, or a little mistaken.

—Jane Austen

"I do *not* wish to be ravished!" I managed to shout in a whisper.

"For a woman who does not want to be ravished, my dear, you are spending an inordinate amount of time staring at my lips."

"I am not staring at your lips!" I said, staring at his lips.

This wasn't going the way I expected, and I was peeved. I tore my gaze away from his mouth and focused upon my hand instead—until I realized with no small amount of horror that my traitorous extremity really belonged to some harlot who was busy stroking lazy circles on the bedpost with the sensitive tip of her middle finger. I snatched it away and tucked both hands behind my back.

"This is-is absurd," I stammered. "What is this claptrap about a grand house party?" I demanded.

He tucked his own hands behind his back and, clearing his throat, walked to the window and stared out at the stars. After a moment, he pulled a golden coin from his pocket and flipped it absently in the air, as though deep in thought. "I find myself in a predicament. My servant ran away."

"Your servant?"

"Yes. My cook."

"Your cook."

He nodded. "Milk leaves me dyspeptic, and my cook accompanies me on my travels."

"Why have I never seen him?"

"Because he is a she. An unmarried young woman, and it would not be proper for her to travel with me unaccompanied. She travels ahead of me, always. But this time, she traveled too far ahead—to Gretna Green, to be precise. With my valet."

"I see. But what about the food here at The Dancing Maiden? You seem quite fond of my cheese pie."

Slowly, he stepped closer to me, until I could feel the warmth of his body. "It is rude," he murmured, "for a man to refuse what a lady offers, the consequences be damned."

I stood my ground. "You, sir, are a rake."

"Then you aren't really offering me anything? Only using your feminine wiles to influence me?"

"My *feminine wiles!*"

"What else would you call it?"

"You are worse than a rake. You are a-a dastard!"

"Undoubtedly. And you, sweet miss, are a flower begging to be plucked."

"I am four-and-twenty, sir. Well past the first blush and quite indifferent to *your* charm."

"You have never been indifferent, not once in the eight years we have known each other."

"I hardly think we know each other."

He cocked his head and threw me a devilish grin. "Not as much as I would wish, no."

"You are no gentleman!"

"I thought we had already established that," he said dryly.

"I had. Long ago." *Change the subject, change the subject!* I spun away from him. "What were you saying about your eloping servants?"

He coughed. "It is a simple arrangement, really. I need a cook, and you need to stay out of trouble. Therefore, I will agree to refrain from calling for a magistrate if you will agree to accompany me to the Earl of Instep's house party as my cook."

"An earl's house! As your cook!"

"You are an expert at cookery, are you not?"

"Yes, but—"

"It is settled then. We leave tomorrow. When we return, all transgressions will be forgotten."

"Which transgressions?" I asked. "Mine, or yours?"

"Why, Miss Grey, your insinuations are shocking! Yours, of course. I say, you *are* very focused upon the idea of transgression. Perhaps if we transgressed a little, you will be more able to concentrate on the business of serving as my cook?"

I pressed my lips together and shook my head. "I will serve as your cook. And gratefully. No *transgression* is necessary."

He chuckled. "I am sorry to hear that."

"How long will I be gone?"

"Only three weeks."

"Three weeks! Out of the question! I have an inn to run."

"Very well," he said, "Then you prefer letting a magistrate settle the matter after all?"

Any moment now, my face was going to freeze into a permanent scowl. "You win," I said. "On one condition."

"You are hardly in a position to negotiate."

"Nevertheless," I said, "I must insist."

"Go on."

"You need a valet, do you not?"

"I have someone in mind."

"So do I."

"Oh?"

"My uncle."

"Your uncle! He is older than God! The idea is absurd."

"He is alert and spry, and I wager he can ride and shoot better than you!"

"That's the way, Leah! Let him have it!" the willowy blonde called from the floor at Erma's feet. "Sic him! Eat him up!"

"Shh!" said another young lady. "Go on, Erma! What did he have to say to that?"

Erma chuckled. She opened the other book. "'No,'" she read. "'Absolutely not. Out of the question. No . . .'"

I watched uncertainty march across Apple's features before her face hardened into stubborn planes.

"Either Uncle comes with us," she said, "or *I* call in the magistrate myself. If my *feminine wiles* do not work on you, perhaps they will on the magistrate!"

By Jove, the stubborn chit meant it!

Now, John Bird was pleasant enough, but he was eighty if he was a day and dotty as they came. It was going to look deuced odd bringing him along to the earl's estate as my valet, but there wasn't a thing I could do about it. I certainly wasn't going to call the chit's bluff and bring in a magistrate.

I'd spent my life avoiding those fine fellows!

And—*hell and blast!*—I certainly had no wish to see anyone jailed, transported, or hung for thievery, least of all Apple. I'd sooner cut off my right hand—which was a weighty thought, for I was the best thief in all England. I'd never been caught. I'd never even been close to being caught, and all I had to do was nip this last prize. I would recover my mother's sapphire at last, and perhaps some knowledge of her fate as well.

And so I resigned myself to the temporary services of

an elderly, somewhat eccentric valet. Of course, I consoled myself with the idea that the delectable Apple wouldn't really be playing the part of cook. No, the delicious Apple's role was to be a much more pleasant one—for both of us. For in order to be quite convincing, we'd have to be caught kissing.

I planned to be caught several times.

I held my breath as a parade of thought shaped Mr. Morgan's features.

"Very well," he finally said. "Your uncle is my new valet, for now. And, perhaps after I have gone you will concede that I am, indeed, a gentleman." He took my hand, brushed his lips across the backs of my fingers, bowed, and left. And then I *did* feel faint. I sat heavily on my bed and laid my hand against my cheek. I could feel the heat there and knew I must look like a giant tomato.

"So much for being ravished," I muttered.

What had I expected?

I'd expected to be taken into his arms and kissed senseless, at the very least. I hadn't wanted to give in to his advances, but he wasn't forcing me—I was the one who had made the offer, after all. He was a man and I couldn't have blamed him for making good on my promise. And as long as I'd had no choice but to be ravished, I had determined that I might as well enjoy the experience, as I would likely never, ever have it again.

Besides . . . Mr. Morgan had always seemed a little . . . well, a little tantalizing, I admit! He wasn't exactly handsome, but those laughingly mischievous, ardently burning blue eyes of his had made more than one appearance in my daydreams.

But ravishment wasn't what was on his mind at all. No, all he wanted was to examine my wardrobe to see if I had anything good enough for a cook to wear. A cook!

I *flumped* back down onto the bed and clutched my

pillow. Instead of his lover, I was now his servant. But I supposed I should be grateful. Things could have turned out much worse. Mr. Morgan was an honorable and good man. He thought I'd tried to steal from him and was willing to overlook the fact in exchange for three weeks' service. I supposed I should be grateful for such a lenient punishment.

I gave my pillow a satisfying *thwack!*

Grateful, hell! I was angry.

I fell asleep, dreaming about ravishment and awakened at sunrise to the cocks crowing outside my window and a puddle of drool on my pillow. Drat, but I hate drool!

As the sun began to pinken the sky, I dressed in the dark blue cotton, packed a small bag, and ate a hasty breakfast while giving instructions to my staff. Uncle John wandered into the kitchen, and I took him aside to explain the situation. To my surprise, he clapped his hands together with glee and trotted upstairs to pack.

"I have never been a valet," he tossed over his shoulder. "I fancy I shall be very bad at it. What fun!"

Suddenly, my heart felt lighter. Uncle always had been able to turn persimmons into pie. Perhaps this miserable adventure wouldn't be so miserable after all. Perhaps I had only to set aside my slightly bruised feminine sensibilities and look on things more positively. I wasn't going to have the adventure of being ravished by the attractive Mr. Morgan, but I *was* going to cook in an earl's kitchen. I wouldn't be allowed out of the servants' areas, but neither would Uncle John, which meant that he would have no opportunity to borrow from the guests, and if I were clever, perhaps I could steal a peek at the rest of the house. An excited shiver ran down my spine. I'd never set foot in a building larger than The Dancing Maiden or grander than the village church. Surely an earl's house would be both, and I would be staying there for an entire fortnight! I was but fourteen when my parents were taken from me, and I'd worked every day since. I worried about what would happen to The Maiden while I was gone, but the servants pished and toshed until they had me mostly convinced they could handle my absence, and I began to feel a little excited anticipation. It was almost like going on holiday, something I'd never dreamed of doing.

The rest of the morning proceeded at a fast pace and finally the three of us—Mr. Morgan, Uncle John, and I—set off in The Maiden's coach-and-four, leading Mr. Morgan's fine black alongside. The crisp morning air held the barest promise of autumn just around the bend, but the rising sun warmed the hills and lazy bees browsed the flowers that edged the lanes. It turned into a glorious summer day, and I was going on an adventure. It was quite simple, really. I was a servant and Mr. Morgan my employer. He'd been but toying with me last night, when he'd led me to believe he wished to have his way with me. It had all been a joke, a hum, a farradiddle. Just like the countless invitations to sit on his lap had been over the years. Nothing had changed between us. We were friends, of a sort. There was no question of ravishment, and there never had been.

We were rolling down the road at a good clip a little after noon when Uncle said around a bite of apple tart, "I am so glad I pinched your sapphire, sir!"

My own tart slid out of my frozen fingers and onto my lap, knocking my entire lunch onto the floor, not that I'd noticed yet.

"You!" Mr. Morgan's eyes flicked my way before returning to Uncle. "*You* took the sapphire from my pocket?"

"Oh, yes," Uncle said proudly. "I am quite good at it—pinching I mean."

"I should say you are!" Mr. Morgan said and leaned forward, his eyes wide with fascination. "I keep a rather close watch over my things. How ever did you manage it?"

"Well," Uncle said, warming to the subject, "I must say it took me years to figure a way to get past your defenses."

He laughed, shaking a finger at Mr. Morgan. "You're a wily one, you are!"

I sat there with my mouth hanging open and my stomach in my throat, while Mr. Morgan hung upon every syllable as he listened to Uncle John tell first how he'd borrowed from Mr. Morgan's pocket and then how he borrowed from everyone else's. He detailed all of his favorite techniques. I tried to busy myself with my remaining lunch—an apple, I was chagrined to find—and I'm sure my skin was flaming as red as the fruit, not that Mr. Morgan noticed, for he was too busy listening to Uncle!

Finally, Mr. Morgan sat back against the threadbare squabs and shook his head in apparent amazement. "You, sir, are truly a great thief!"

I almost choked. "How dare you call my uncle a thief!" I cried. "He is no more a thief than I am!"

Mr. Morgan blinked and looked over at me. Clearly, he'd almost forgotten I was there, the wretch! "Beg pardon?"

"Uncle does not steal; he borrows." I explained about the diagram.

"So you were trying to *return* my sapphire, not steal it?"

I rolled my eyes. "Yesss!" I said, as though he were the stupidest man in all England.

"And when I accused you of trying to steal it, you took the blame to protect Mr. Bird."

"Please," I said. "This doesn't change anything, does it? You will hold to our bargain, will you not?"

He looked offended. "Of course I will."

Still, I persisted. "May I have your word on it, sir?"

"You have my word," he said with a mischievous chuckle and a flash of dimples. *"As a gentleman."*

That did it. I couldn't be peeved with him any more, not in the face of such unflagging good humor, and once more we shared a smile. It felt good.

We stopped for lunch at a small inn that was little more

than a roadside tavern. The tables were wobbly, the ale poor, and the stables encrusted with years of filth.

"Your place is so far superior that I wonder how this place stays in business," Mr. Morgan whispered to me as we waited in the tiny common room for meat pies, apple tarts, and ale to be brought out.

"It appears to be the only choice. There has been nothing for six miles."

"And there is nothing for another six miles. In comparison, your village is a thriving city. I fancy The Dancing Maiden is the heart of your village. You should be proud of it."

"I am." I wasn't ashamed to admit it. "My father opened The Maiden the year he wed my mother. They both worked hard."

"As do you."

I did not deny it. "There is no shame in honest toil."

"I did not intend to imply there was."

It was an uncomfortable little moment, and I craned my neck, looking for Uncle. "Just how far away is the necessary?"

"Worried that your uncle will get lost?"

"He is not that old and dotty!"

"You are determined to think the worst of me," he said. "I did not say he was old and dotty. On the contrary, any man who can pick my pocket is cunning and quick!"

I bit my lip.

"Why is your forehead all wrinkly, Apple?"

"I worry a little about what will happen at the earl's house party. What if Uncle borrows things while I'm busy cooking?"

"Do not fret. Even if he does take something, I wager he will not be caught, and we will return the things." He smiled and shook his head. "Your uncle is really quite an amazingly accomplished pickpocket!"

"La!" I cried. "Will you stop that?"

"What?"

"Calling my uncle a thief! He isn't a thief, I tell you. He does not steal things. We have never once kept anything he has borrowed. We give them back. Always. He has no intention of keeping the things he borrows, so you cannot possibly call him a thief!"

"All right! All right!" He held up his palms. "Calm yourself! What is it you hold against thieves, anyway? Has The Maiden been robbed or something?"

I looked away. It was enough to have to live with the memory. To speak of it was too painful.

"Thieves are evil," I said at last, "and that is that. You do not have to be a saint to know that. I have every blasted right to defend my uncle's honor, sir! Please do not pester me with questions. Where there are flowers there are bees. My guests all have money to spend, and thieves are never far away."

"Again, I have managed to prick your temper."

Just then, a woman who could only be described as a wench brought the food. Mr. Morgan paid, and we took our meal outside. The air inside the inn was stale, and there was a fine, warm breeze sifting through the trees outside.

The rest of the day was quite uneventful until evening, when we stopped at a lovely old inn for the night. I thought it strange I'd never heard of The Birdhouse before—until I discovered just what sort of birds it housed!

"The Birdhouse?" the youngest of the ladies cried. Barely eighteen, she was clearly surprised, though some of the others had already guessed what was coming and smiled at her naïveté. "Did she mean here? Where we live? Right here?"

"Right here." Erma nodded.

"What happened when she went inside?"

"I'll bet she peed her pants," said the blonde.

"Do be proper!" said another. "Wager. The proper term is wager!"

All the ladies laughed.

"Did they wear panties back then?" asked a short, brown-eyed beauty.

"I wouldn't," the blonde answered. "Not around Mr. Morgan!" That quip had the girls clutching their bellies and howling.

"Ladies!" Erma cried. "I see it is late and we are punchy. Perhaps we have somewhere else to be? Like bed?"

That straightened them up. They sobered immediately, and one said in a very proper voice, "We apologize, Erma. Do go on."

"Very well. Now, where was I? Oh yes . . ."

CHAPTER FOUR

The pot calls the pan burnt-arse.

—John Clarke

Birds of paradise, ladybirds, high flyers—I was surrounded by prostitutes the moment I set foot in the door. Or, more accurately, Mr. Morgan was surrounded.

They rushed over to him in a silken cloud of perfumed glory. Blondes, reds, and chestnuts—even a pair of white-haired beauties. They were quite friendly, and I was appalled. Clearly they all knew him. Clearly, they all liked him.

Clearly, I was enraged.

The rake had tried to kiss me that morning, blast him! And I was going to let him, blast him! What did he think I was, some lightskirt?

"Oh, Pos!" the blondest said with a pretty pout. "You have been away so long!"

"Naughty, naughty boy," a brunette said. "Mama spank!"

Mr. Morgan held up his hands. "Surely you will refrain from beating me until after I have given you your presents."

"Do leave him alone, ladies!" another cried.

All the ladies trilled with laughter.

A tall woman glanced at Uncle John and me. "But who

are these delightful creatures?" she asked with a light French accent and moved to take first my hand and then John's. She was not a young woman. Her red hair was shot with gray, but she was still striking, something Uncle John evidently noticed at once. Bending over her hand, he performed a ritual kiss and murmured, "Enchanté, madam."

I could only gape.

Mr. Morgan stepped up. "Miss Constance Cherry, I have the rare pleasure of introducing you to my dear friends, Mr. John Bird and his niece Miss Leah Grey."

Black eyes demurely lowered, spine straight, and grace showing in every movement, Miss Cherry performed a perfect curtsy. "I am honored. Will we have the pleasure of your company until tomorrow? And dare we hope that you will extend your stay?"

Mr. Morgan gave a surprisingly delicate cough. "We will stay the entire three days I promised, *mon cher*," he said quietly.

Another round of excited comment followed this pronouncement, but Miss Cherry quelled the younger women with a stern look. "Ladies. I believe you all have other places to be?"

The "ladies" quit the room, casting fond looks at Mr. Morgan and curious ones at Uncle and me.

Being the daughter of an innkeeper, rather than the daughter of a duke, my education did not have the blind spots under which young ladies from Polite Society labored. I knew young men generally did not *stay* in such houses overnight. Yet Mr. Morgan had not only planned to sleep there for three nights, but also written ahead to inform them of that fact. To call him a regular customer, I realized, was probably an understatement. And to call me dismayed definitely was!

I don't know which bothered me more: the fact that he frequented a brothel, the fact that he thought it was acceptable to bring us along with him, or the fact that I was a wee little touch jealous of all the little birdies!

Wee little touch, my fanny, I thought. *You're as green-eyed as they come.*

My eyes returned from a roll around their sockets just as Miss Cherry turned back to us, and her face broke into a smile. "Callahan," she addressed the footman. "Please bring in our guests' bags."

"'Ere now, I'll help wi' that," Uncle John said and bustled off after the footman.

I held up my hand. "But—"

Miss Cherry laid one hand over mine and put one finger of the other to her lips.

"He suffers dreadfully from rheumatism in this weather," I said after Uncle was gone. "He should not be allowed to—"

"Miss Cherry is right, my dear," said Mr. Morgan quietly. "Rheumatism comes and goes, but if you take away a man's dignity, it is gone forever."

Miss Cherry nodded with a soft smile. "I will inform Cook there will be three more for supper." She turned to me. "What a delight to have you here! We must trade stories over tea. I daresay Posthumous will have no more secrets before we are through." She grinned in Mr. Morgan's direction.

"Posthumous?" I asked. "Do you mean Mr. Morgan?"

For a split second, Miss Cherry's face went blank, but then she laughed and said. "Yes, of course. It is our little—how do you say it?—our *hum,* the name we call him." She turned away, too quickly. "And now you will like to refresh yourselves." She rang a little silver bell and a maid appeared instantly. "Sophia, please show Miss Grey to the Swallows. Mr. Bird will be most comfortable in the Blackbird, I think. And the Peacock is for P-ah . . . *Mr. Morgan,* as always."

Sophia nodded. "This way, if you please. Though we do not entertain town guests, we do town hours and dine at ten," she said, moving off toward the wide, elegant marble stairs.

I threw a speaking glance at Mr. Morgan. *Peacock?* I mouthed.

He bowed deeply and used his hands to mime an imaginary tail spread wide above his trim bottom before looking up at me with a mischievous grin. *At your service,* he mouthed.

I couldn't help the bubble of laughter that welled up, and, though I tried to keep it in check, I fear I let go a very unladylike snort. Covering my mouth, I rolled my eyes yet again, and he gave a bark of unrestrained laughter, while Miss Cherry glanced back just in time to see a smile commandeer my face. I did my best to steel my expression, but she looked from me to Mr. Morgan and back again before raising one speculative eyebrow and then looking away.

"I believe you will find your room warm enough," she said over her shoulder, "but if not, do feel free to seek another. I am afraid you will have to rely upon yourself for that, however, for we will have no other . . . visitors these three days, and apart from a pair of watchmen, our servants are all abed between the hours of midnight and four-o'-the-clock."

Her meaning was quite clear, and I was glad I was behind her, for I felt my skin flame red. I could feel Mr. Morgan's eyes boring into my back, and just as I turned the corner on the landing, I ventured a glance at him. He was watching me, all right. But he was no longer smiling. Instead, he was staring at me with a decidedly masculine intensity.

I shivered and stepped around the corner, feeling as though the world was spinning around me. His flirtation wasn't a game, I realized. It wasn't an idle diversion. It wasn't a hum. Nor an act of mercy to flatter the spinster innkeeper.

No. Mr. Morgan's interest in me was *real!*

When had that happened? And how had I missed it?

The next few minutes I hardly remember. I was shown

to my room and a maid helped me undress and wash. I
was given a wrapper to put on while my own gown was
freshened, and I lay down.

Feigning deep sleep, I skipped supper. I and my complaining stomach lay in the sumptuous bed of the Swallows
room, staring at the looping, wheeling birds painted across
the faux clouds on the ceiling and wondering how I'd let
myself come to this. To be sleeping in a brothel under the
same roof as a man who wanted to . . . to ravish me!

It wasn't that I was worried for my reputation. An
innkeeper's daughter hardly has any reputation to protect, and I had absolutely none at all. A woman in trade
was highly suspect, and I regularly committed the social
sin of speaking with strangers from all rungs on the
social ladder. Heaven only knew what sorts of things I'd
learned! Almost everyone viewed me variously as a possible swindler, a bawd, or a fancy piece. At the very least
I was privy to subjects no true lady would ever know.

Apparently, though, I hadn't learned enough to satisfy
me.

I lay awake until the morning hours, dwelling ridiculously upon the notion that any competent innkeeper
ought to know all there was to know on the subject of ravishment. Instead, here I was a maiden of twenty-and-
four who hadn't even been kissed.

The women of The Birdhouse probably hadn't been
kissed, either. No, they probably did the kissing all themselves! How many of them had kissed Mr. Morgan? Was
one of them kissing him right then? At that very moment?
I punched my pillow and turned over with a sigh.

It wasn't my concern.

Downstairs, a clock struck the hours with maddening
regularity until finally at three-o'-the-clock I rose and
barricaded the door with my delicate dressing table, a
wing chair, and a heavy washstand, just to be sure I could
not walk in my sleep in search of a *warmer* chamber. And
then, after several more satisfying blows to my hapless

pillow, I drifted off and dreamed of peacocks skulking outside my door, whereas Mr. Morgan probably . . .

. . . went to sleep immediately and awakened refreshed
just after dawn, having dreamed of Apple, of course.
After a good, hard ride, I washed and dressed with care
and then spent the morning visiting with the ladies. It was
good to see them. I'd been gone almost a year this time,
and there were two new faces, as Bernadette, I was pleased
to learn, had left to begin a new life in the Colonies, and
Hazel had married The Birdhouse's gardener and now
lived in relative respectability in a cottage upon the
grounds. She was expecting her first child in early winter.

It was always good to come home, as I thought of The
Birdhouse and its pleasant little village, Blackthorn. My
mother had walked its narrow lanes and over its green
meadows, and I always felt closer to her when I was there.
It was a bittersweet thing, though, and already this morning I felt restless, a feeling perhaps made worse by the con-
spicuous absence of Constance Cherry. I relied upon
her wise counsel, her understanding, and her forgiveness,
for she alone knew what and who I really was—and what
I was not.

Whether I cared to admit it or not, I was nervous about
the coming house party, and I wanted to speak to her
about it, but I hadn't so much as a glimpse of her all morning until close on midday. I was standing alone in the library,
toying with my medallion when I spied a flash of blue out
the window. She was walking outdoors with John Bird.
Their steps bespoke of unhurried leisure, and their heads
were bent close together as they talked. As I watched, Constance tipped her head up in laughter before brushing one
tender hand over Mr. Bird's shoulder, and he trapped her
fingers in his own and kissed them.

Stunned, I turned from the window only to discover
Apple standing behind me, her eyes wide. She opened her

mouth and then closed it again before gesturing in the air. "I have never seen him like that. With anyone." She shook her head disbelievingly.

"Nor I her. Their *tendre* is surprising."

"And devilish quick, don't you think?"

Her sharp tone surprised me. "I should think that at his age he knows his own mind and heart. Who are we to question the connection?"

"But you *are* questioning?" she asked.

"I have known Constance—Miss Cherry—for a long time. She is a wise and good woman, and no one deserves happiness more than she, but that she should find it with John Bird seems . . . unlikely."

Miss Grey's face flushed pink. "And may I ask what is wrong with Mr. Bird?"

Nothing was wrong with Mr. Bird. All I meant was that the pair were so different one from the other, but Apple didn't give me a chance to explain before waggling her finger, scowling, and ringing a peal over my head.

"I'll have you know, Mr. Morgan, that my uncle is as wise and as good as your Miss Cherry! Even if you still harbor the ridiculous notion that he is a thief, you must own that he is at least as honorable as a common prostitute!"

I have never been more angry with anyone than I was at that moment. "There is nothing common about Constance Cherry, and being a-a prostitute and being a lady are not mutually exclusive."

"Perhaps not, but it is still wrong."

"Right, wrong—bah! There is no right and wrong. No black and white. The world is made up of shades of gray."

"With people like you in it, yes," she said. "People like you force shades of gray upon people like me."

"What?"

"Well, look at you!" She made a sweeping gesture from my head to my toes. "Today, you are turned out like any young buck of the *ton*. Embroidered waistcoat, perfectly tied cravat. Right down to the silver buckles on your shoes. You, sir, are wealthy."

"What has that to do with—"

"Wealthy! Yet for years you have been sallying about the countryside pretending to be a poor workingman—God only knows why!—and you would have gone on fooling me had I not found out about that sapphire in your pocket!"

"Which your uncle stole."

"Borrowed."

"Oh, I understand now! I was wrong about you."

"Thank you," she said, primly.

"You *do* see shades of gray—but only when you choose to see them. You, Miss Grey, are a hypocrite."

Her mouth dropped open. "Knowing the difference between right and wrong does not make one a hypocrite! You are the hypocrite here! Walking around with a sapphire the size of Windsor Castle in your tattered pocket!"

"I, at least, know better than to judge people by the way they are forced to feed themselves, rather than by the strength of their character. Constance has welcomed you into her home with unconditional hospitality. How can you stand there and condemn her? You don't even know her!"

"But you do. Intimately, I assume."

"Ooo . . ." breathed the brown-eyed young woman. "She stepped in it that time!"

"Don't be vulgar, Allison. But you are right. Leah did err." Switching to Leah's journal, she read on . . .

I watched his face compress into angry lines, and then he straightened, raised his chin a notch, and addressed me in a quiet, aloof manner that chilled me to the bone.

"Your assumptions do not concern me, Miss Grey. It is what you make of them that sickens me." With that, he quit the room, leaving me to struggle with an amorphous shame that swirled and tangled with morality in my head. Rubbish! He was just twisting words. I hadn't insulted Miss Cherry. Not really. I had merely stated fact. She was a common prostitute—or a bawd, which was surely worse.

Wasn't it?

I groaned and, crossing my arms over my chest, stomped back and forth across the library floor a few times. The dratted man had me questioning my own morals! What was next?

I didn't have a chance to sort it all out before a clatter of hooves at the front of the house drew my attention. A glimpse out the library window yielded a half-dozen small carts. A flotilla of women spilled forth—seamstresses, judging by the measuring tapes, pattern books, bolts of cloth, and chatelaines they carried toward the house.

Someone cleared her throat at the library door. "They're here, miss!"

It was the maid Sophia. I gave her a quizzical look.

"The dressmakers," she prompted. "Did Pos not—ah, Mr. Morgan, that is!—did he not tell you?"

I shook my head.

"Well, 'tis no matter. Come along!"

I followed her into a large morning parlor where the apparent commander of the navy, a small woman with gray hair, nimble fingers, and sharp eyes, assembled her fleet and planned her attack. It didn't take me long to discover the fact that *I* was the one to be conquered!

"There has been some mistake," I protested. "I did not order a new gown."

"*A* new gown!" Sophia laughed. "These ladies are here to make you a complete wardrobe."

"I did not ask them to come!"

"I know."

"But, Sophia, I cannot afford even *one* gown!" I cried before a sudden suspicion gripped my heart and squeezed. "Oh, la! You do not think I am . . . that I have become . . . that I am now *living* here, do you?"

The younger woman laughed. "*You?* Pish-tosh! Heavens no! My dear Miss Grey, it was Pos who sent for the dressmakers. He has ordered dresses, hats, new chemises—"

"What need have I of all that?"

Sophia eyed my blue cotton and bit her lip. "Your clothes are . . . a little worn, don't you think?" she asked politely.

I subsided, knowing she was right. My clothes *were* unsuitable. For anything. The few gowns I owned had belonged to my mother. Fifteen years out of fashion, faded, and thin, they'd been repaired so many times that I looked more like a scarecrow than a young lady—or even like a wealthy man's servant.

"How much is this likely to cost?" I asked. I had some savings tucked away, and the thought of a pair of new gowns was appealing. Besides, I reasoned, it would reflect well upon The Dancing Maiden to have its proprietor respectably gowned. Mayhap I wouldn't have my bottom pinched as often!

"Very well," I said with a little shrug. "So long as the expense does not go beyond ten pounds."

Sophia exchanged looks with the Admiral.

"I am still to send him the bill?" the Admiral asked.

Sophia nodded. "He is a generous man, and he left strict instructions that Miss Grey be gowned befitting a man of his station. If I were you"—she turned to me with a mischievous glint in her eyes—"I would endeavor not to disappoint him." She winked and turned to smooth her hand worshipfully over a bolt of rose silk. "I should think he would be very satisfied to see you in yards and yards of this, for instance! It is very expensive, I am sure. Only think how pleased he will be when he receives the bill!"

"This is so fancy!" I said, fingering the silk. "A cook would never wear this."

Sophia laughed. "Indeed, not! My advice to you, my dear Miss Grey, is to enjoy yourself."

She left the room, and I watched her go, thinking

hard as the navy began measuring and arranging fashion plates and fabrics and trimmings about the room to show them to their best advantage.

I didn't know how to feel. I'd hardly ever had new clothes, and the sumptuous silks, delicate laces, and translucent lawns before me almost made my mouth water, but it had been presumptuous indeed for Mr. Morgan to order a new wardrobe without consulting me. I did need the clothes, both for my role as his cook and for my role as proprietress of The Maiden, but my pride demanded that I pay for the lot myself.

I was still seething from our argument of a few minutes before. Even if I did pay for the clothing, the wretch would probably expect me to be grateful for his intervention!

"How much did Mr. Morgan say he would pay for a new wardrobe?" I asked the Admiral.

"He did not say, miss. He only gave us a list of the items you were to have and said you should choose whatever styles you wanted so long as they were the best."

Sophia's advice echoed in my head. *Enjoy yourself.*

I certainly will! I thought with a soft chuckle. To the devil with pride. I would make the wealthy Mr. Morgan wish he had been a little more mannerly to me this morning! I allowed the measuring to continue, smiling the while until I remembered something else Sophia had said.

Aside from my embarrassing lack of empirical knowledge about ravishment, I asked myself, just what was so improbable about the notion of me becoming one of Miss Cherry's birds?

I wasn't hideous, but even a swan, plucked clean of feathers, would be ugly. Perhaps a little plumage would improve my aspect. A bright yet serviceable calico or two would do very—

Calico, my foot! Serviceable my eye! For once, I wasn't going to do the practical thing. Floating silks, delicate lawns, sheer muslins. Lilac and rose, sky-blue and daffodil.

I'd never thought I'd have such fine garments—but I'd daydreamed of it, and Mr. Morgan, the pompous rake, owed me.

Lust after me and then call me a hypocrite, would he?

And maybe—just maybe—if the Admiral were skilled enough, and the candlelight low enough and I looked through my eyelashes and batted them just right, Mr. Morgan would soon be the one punching his pillow and staring at his ceiling at night.

CHAPTER FIVE

The constancy of the wise is nothing else but the knack of concealing their passion and trouble.
— François, Duc De La Rochefoucauld

Choosing a new wardrobe was four hours of hard work, and the Admiral was a termagant! I was ready to keelhaul her after the first hour. By the time she and her navy left, I was at wit's end.

Next came a most uncomfortable tea.

At The Dancing Maiden, I knew how to make small talk, but at The Birdhouse I was sunk. I could not inquire after a lady's relations, home life, ancestry, occupation, education, or anything else that related to her past history. Nor could I politely ask after her future plans without implying that her current circumstances were less than perfect. Fashion was too trivial, politics too controversial. I was limited to the weather, which was uncooperatively fine at present and therefore not of much interest. It was all devilishly awkward!

Fortunately, one of the seamstresses had left behind her sewing basket, which gave me the perfect excuse for escaping The Birdhouse. Tying on my old, worn chip bonnet, I sailed into the afternoon sunshine with the sewing basket, very grateful to be free, and headed for the largish village of Blackthorn, a half-league away.

Apart from a half-dozen provisioning trips to the market fair with my parents, I'd never spent time away from The Dancing Maiden. Never had I lingered in a village other than my own tiny one, and I was eager to see what Blackthorn was like.

Besides, the less time I spent inside The Birdhouse, the better. It wasn't that the ladies were unpleasant. No, they were disconcertingly pleasant. They were polite and well-spoken, too. They weren't what I'd expected of prostitutes. I began to wonder if Mr. Morgan had been right. Had I misjudged the women of The Birdhouse?

No. I shook my head. One could gild a chunk of coal, but that didn't make it gold. One could teach a woman manners, but that did not change who she was inside—and what sort of woman chose to make her living like that, when she could become a servant in some house or a servingmaid like my Betsy or Anne back at The Dancing Maiden?

I set the matter aside and tried to enjoy the walk. Mr. Morgan was entitled to his opinions, but I wasn't going to let him force them upon me. I might have to conform to his demands for the next three weeks, but I didn't have to conform to his values. I took a deep breath and thought no more of it.

The day was fine and the walk to Blackthorn pleasant. A brisk wind carried a faint tang of the sea. My footsteps' steady rhythm was reassuring. Walking always felt good like that—predictable, measured, unsurprising. This was no different, just a normal walk into a normal village. Nothing surprising there.

I should have known better.

As I walked past an outlying farm, I was accosted by a mermaid!

"Hullo!" she sang out, and I whirled around. She was a beauty. About ten years old with long blond hair and a sprinkling of freckles. She was attempting to climb over a stile without much success.

"Can you help me please, miss? My tail is caught." She frowned and pointed to her legs, which were encased in a tube of gray-green cloth.

I lifted her down easily, but the costume had ripped a little, and she frowned. "I shouldn't have put it on yet," she said, "but I just couldn't wait. It is so pretty. Do you not think so?"

"Oh . . . yes, indeed. You are without doubt the most beautiful mermaid I have ever seen on an English country lane."

She wrinkled her nose. "Really?"

"Really." I nodded.

"Where are you from?" she asked abruptly.

"I am staying . . . nearby," I said carefully.

She looked down the lane the direction I'd come. "Nothing out that way but The Birdhouse. Are you staying there?"

I nodded. "My, but it is a lovely day, is it not?"

"My mama stayed there, too."

"Oh?" I managed.

The mermaid nodded. "Before she met my father, it was. Miss Cherry gave her this when she left there," she said proudly, pulling at a chain that hung round her neck. A little gold medallion appeared in her hand. As she held it up for me to see, the sun glinted on the wings of a bird worked onto its surface. "She lets us girls wear it sometimes. On special days."

"Is today a special day?"

She gifted me with a pretty smile and nodded.

"Where are you headed?" Dressed as she was, I was afraid her "special day" might include a paddle in the sea, which wasn't more than four or five leagues away. If she made it there, she'd drown, dressed as she was—though I didn't see how she could get there, since she couldn't even get down from the stile unassisted. Still . . .

"I am going to the village," she said, relieving my anxiety. "Pageant practice begins today. Vicar Sweet said we were to bring in costumes."

"Costumes? For a Christmas pageant, is it?"

The little girl nodded her head, and then a pained expression contorted her pixie features. "Is Bethlehem near the ocean?"

"I do not know," I lied.

"This costume is all I had," she said. "A traveling show left it behind last winter."

It wasn't hard to see why. The costume was ragged and worn. The once-green tail had faded almost to gray. It wasn't worth saving, even for scraps.

"I wanted to be an angel." She dashed at the tear that formed in her eye, and an idea popped into my head. I nodded at the little farmhouse.

"Is that where you live?" I asked.

Her chin rose. "That is the Brown farm," she said proudly. "I am Miss Sarah Elizabeth Violet Brown." She curtsied.

"I am Miss Leah Grey, and I am delighted to meet you, Miss Brown."

"It's Miss Sarah," she said. "I have one older sister and six younger ones—and then there are my brothers." She wrinkled her nose again. "No time for making costumes at my house. Everyone has more important things to do."

And with a family so large, no extra cloth to be had, either, I was sure. "Well, Miss Sarah, it seems you have a problem. I have one too. Perhaps we can help each other. This basket, you see, is very heavy. If you will carry it into Blackthorn for me. . . ."

"Uh-oh . . . she's going to get into some kind of trouble in the village, I know it!" Allison remarked.

"It's not Leah who finds trouble in the village," Erma said. "It's our Mr. Morgan." The pronouncement extracted oohs and ahhs from her audience, and she went on reading. "'An hour and a half later, we . . .'"

. . . parted company. Miss Sarah was late to pageant practice, but I doubted the Vicar Sweet would mind very much. The little girl's eyes shone almost as brightly as her new silver wings. The seamstress had been grateful to have her basket back before Admiral Termagant found out it was gone, and she'd been very happy to do me a favor, especially after I offered her a coin or two. The costume she'd concocted for Miss Sarah was lovely. The pageant would have a very beautiful angel indeed. I smiled after the girl as she skipped off happily toward the church.

Suddenly, a familiar figure emerged from one of the tidy little shops. Mr. Morgan. And in his hands he held a small bottle.

I didn't hail him. I was feeling a little guilty, truth to tell, for even if he'd been surly and unreasonable during our argument, I'd behaved badly too, and I knew it. As I watched, he tried to find a pocket for the bottle, but it was soon clear that his pockets were all too small. He sighed and struck off down the lane just as the baker's wife emerged from the bakery.

"Good afternoon, Mrs. Wentworth!" he greeted her.

"Mr. Jones! How lovely to see you again sir!"

Jones?

They chatted for a few moments, and then he tipped his hat, gave a little bow, and started walking again, but he hadn't taken ten steps before another villager hailed him. "Why, bless me!" the man called from across the street. "If it isn't Mr. Jones! Good day to you sir. Well met!" It seemed his voice hadn't finished echoing before a small crowd formed, the women smiling fondly while the men pumped his hand.

I melted into the shadows between two buildings and watched. "Mr. Jones" smiled broadly, clapped several shoulders, and even kissed a new baby! I stared in amazement at the villagers' deference. Finally, the group dispersed, and the object of their admiration strode off down the lane once more.

I fell into step beside him. "It seems you are a popular man here in Blackthorn. You have them charmed, just as you do back at The Maiden."

He buffed his nails upon his blue superfine coat with mock superiority. "They love me. Everyone does. I cannot deny it."

I laughed before I remembered I was still miffed with him. "You are outrageous."

"Thank you." He tipped his tall hat and sketched a bow.

We walked on in silence for a time, and then I said, "Jack Morgan or Posthumous Jones?"

He gave me a wry smile. "You noticed that, did you?"

"The crowd of people calling their hullos was difficult to miss," I said. "So . . . which is it?"

He hesitated the barest fraction of a second. "Both, actually."

"And that business of calling you Posthumous being all a hum?"

"A ruse. My real name is Posthumous Jones."

"Then who is Jack Morgan and why is he such a popular and famous personage in Blackthorn village?"

"Jack Morgan is someone I do not want you to mention outside of The Dancing Maiden."

It was clear he would offer no further explanation, and we walked on silently until we were within sight of The Birdhouse. "You can trust me with your secret," I said suddenly.

"I know."

I looked at him quizzically, raising one eyebrow. "You are awfully sure of yourself."

"One can afford to be," he said, "when one is in possession of another's secrets. It seems we are at an impasse,

Apple. I know your uncle pilfers trinkets, and you know
I have a secret identity."

"Stalemate," I agreed.

"You play chess, do you?"

"Think me a lack-wit, do you?" I shot back.

"Far from it, Apple, and that is only one of the many
things I admire about you. I am predisposed to like you,
because I fancy we are alike in many ways. We both live
by our wits. Chess is a mirror of our lives. I suppose you
will want me to take you back to The Dancing Maiden
forthwith, now that I no longer have the advantage?"

I shook my head. "A bargain is a bargain," I said. "It
would be wrong of me to go back on my word."

Out of the corner of my eye I saw the barest hint of a satisfied smile shape his mouth. "Right and wrong," he murmured. "Black and white. Back to that again, are we?"

"Some of us have never left."

"Touché!"

"He took a deep breath. "So. What brought you into
Blackthorn today?"

I explained about the sewing basket. ". . . and then I met
the most darling little girl. Miss Sarah Brown is her name."

He smiled. "Ah, yes. A sweet child."

"You know her?" I asked and then held up my palm.
"Never mind. I forgot; you know everyone here, for you
have spent much time in Blackthorn Village," I probed.
"Is that not so?"

"I take it you enjoyed your coze with Miss Sarah?" he
asked, ignoring my question completely. I decided to let
him get away with it.

"Indeed"—I nodded—"I found her very pleasant. And
much more informative than you." He threw me an arch
look, and I laughed and told him about the rest of our
town adventure. "She said her mother had lived at The
Birdhouse."

He nodded. "She was one of Constance's stray puppies."

"Stray puppies?"

"I thought you weren't a lack-wit, Apple. Have you not comprehended that Constance runs a rescue operation? She takes in strays and finds them suitable homes."

"For puppies?" I said, pretending to be confused.

He laughed again, a rich, frothy sound that made me feel good down to the tips of my tingly toes. "I deserve that," he said.

"The Birdhouse is a home for stray ladies—or perhaps I should say 'ladies who have strayed.'" Constance hand-picks them. Scours the cities for ladies in distress whose hearts are yet true. She is a wise woman. She can see into their souls, I fancy, and she chooses the most deserving to take under her wing. They don't have to be beautiful or young, only *good*, and then, once she has them installed in The Birdhouse, she preens them, refines them, in the hope that, eventually, she can set them free to fly on their own."

"You mean she finds them husbands?"

"Sometimes," he acknowledged. "They are taught how to keep house if they do not already know. But they are also taught to read and write, to sew and to serve, to play music, to speak French, to dance and draw—all the womanly arts. Constance teaches them as much as they will learn. Before the Terror, she was a comtesse who lived a life of grace and ease among the aristocracy of France. Indeed, all of Europe. But her entire family was taken prisoner and executed."

"Oh, no!"

"She alone of her family escaped, and all she came away with was her life. All of their lands and property were forfeit." He stopped suddenly, and I was forced to stop, too. "Constance has many old friends here in England," he said with an uncanny intensity, "both French and English. The Devonshires, the Marlboroughs, the loftiest of the lofties. They would be glad to see her. Among them, she could return to the sort of life she used to lead, if she wished. She was beautiful and of noble birth, and even penniless as she was, she could have made a good match with such friends to recommend her." He toyed with the small coin in his hand, something I was coming to understand as an anxious habit.

"I do not understand. What keeps her here, then?"

"Integrity." He started walking, and I hurried to follow.

"Tell me more. Please," I added. "I would like to know. I would be honored to know."

He gave me an assessing look and then sighed and put the coin back in his pocket. "She was on her way to a friend's house," he said, "somewhere near Portsmouth, when her coach was beset by highwaymen."

"Oh, la! What happened?"

"They forced the coach off the road and into a copse, shot and robbed Constance and her coachman, and left them both for dead. Her man perished, but Constance dragged herself back to the road before she collapsed and was found the next morning."

"Thieves!" I spat. "May they all burn in hell!" My vehemence must have startled Mr. Morgan, for he looked at me rather oddly, and to my own surprise, I was tempted to let go the story of the terrible day my parents died, but at the last moment I looked away. This was not my story, but Miss Cherry's. And I had a feeling that Mr. Morgan needed to tell it.

"Who found her?" I asked.

"The former proprietress of The Birdhouse. She nursed Constance during a fearful fever and a long convalescence. A friendship was forged between them during that time, and they became inseparable friends."

"A young comtesse and an old bawd? How odd!"

"So it would seem," he said, "on the surface. But the old woman and Constance actually had much in common. They were both the daughters of gentlemen who had lost first their fortunes and then their lives. They'd both lost their parents, their friends, and their ways of life. They each understood what the other had endured.

"Fate brought them both to The Birdhouse, and though

Constance never . . . never *made her living* there, she did not condemn her friend for having done so. Instead, she sympathized, empathized—and she never left. Instead, she all but disappeared from Polite Society. She started calling herself 'Miss Cherry,' because her friend had taken to calling her 'cherie.' And she concealed her whereabouts and, except for written correspondence, she gave up her former friends."

"Why? I daresay she is not the only noblewoman to have mixed with people of questionable backgrounds." It had always struck me as ironic that Her Ladyship could invite scoundrels of every description to her parlor and the gathering would be called a "salon," while if a poor commoner did the same, it was a mob.

"By that time, her friend had become ill, and Constance became the acting . . . *proprietor* of The Birdhouse. She realized she had the skills to help the ladies who worked there, and it became her mission to free as many as she could. As of this year, eighty-one have fledged."

"So many!"

"Constance passes her own fine education on to the ladies, teaching them herself, and then she uses her old connections within Society to find them positions as ladies' maids or companions among the *ton*."

"What happened to her friend?"

"She died and left The Birdhouse to Constance. She has been here ever since. Close on forty years."

I shook my head in wonder. "She is an extraordinary woman. I am humbled."

He nodded, and a warm, approving smile shaped his features. "You aren't so terrible either, apart from that nasty tendency you have to judge people before you get to know them."

"Oh, dear." I pinched the bridge of my nose. "What a prig I must seem!"

"I admit I wondered whether I'd misjudged you. But you've spoilt your budding reputation as a prig this morning, I am afraid, for that was a very nice thing you did for our local mermaid."

"It felt nice," I said. "I wish I could see her in the pageant at Christmastime."

Sunlight glinted off the golden coin as he flipped the coin into the air and then slipped it back into his pocket. "Can you not?"

I shook my head. "The Maiden cannot possibly spare me. Christmas is one of our busiest times of year." I bent to snatch a sheaf of grass from the roadside and then worried the hapless blades between my fingers. It had suddenly occurred to me that I'd always be busy at Christmas, that I'd never have time for pageants, that I'd always be working, and I was a little sad and didn't know why I should be. After all, it was a virtue to be steadfastly busy.

"Are you always so responsible?" he asked, strangely mirroring my thoughts.

"I try to be. Mary Wollstonecraft wrote that 'Operations of judgement—'"

"'—are cool and circumspect,'" he finished.

"*You* have read Mary Wollstonecraft?"

"You are not the only one who can read, by Jove, so stop looking at me as though I am some sort of hairy, uncouth beast, and finish the quotation."

"I do not remember it."

"Horse dung! Finish the quotation!"

I threw him a fistful of daggers and pressed my lips together.

He laughed, looked up at the sky, and recited, "'Operations of judgement are cool and circumspect, while coolness and deliberation are great enemies to enthusiasm.' I believe those were her exact words." Raising his chin to a ridiculously high angle, he buffed his nails on his coat, but then spoilt the effect with a sidelong grin.

"Show-off!" I threw my handful of mangled grass at him.

"How can you say such a thing?" he asked.

We walked on saying nothing for a while. He plucked

a blade of grass from his sleeve and, with a happy, care-free zest, made a grass whistle of it and blew a long, rau-cous note across the fields, chuckling when the birds scolded him in return and then giving me a sidelong glance. "Seriously, Apple, you cannot think enthusiasm evil. Do you?"

"No, of course not, but"—the morning had grown warm, and I raked my fingers across my brow, pulling stray hairs from my forehead—"surely you aren't suggesting re-sponsibility is a bad thing!"

"Indeed, not," he replied, "only that occasional *ir*re-sponsibility is more fun."

"You are outrageous!"

And you, my dear Apple, are one starched-up spinster! She was in need of someone to knock her off that oh-so-proper pedestal of hers.

I'd have wagered a single, wild, impetuous kiss would do it. One kiss, and she'd toss *coolness* and *deliberation* to the wolves.

I looked away from her and took a deep breath. I was spending entirely too much time thinking about kissing her. It was natural enough that the thought should cross my mind. A man would have to be dead not to see Apple for the ripe, sweet, juicy little thing she was. It was fine for me to think about plucking her from the tree once in a while, but the truth of it was I'd been thinking of little else since our kiss was interrupted two days before! It had gone beyond a passing thought to a near obsession, and I could not afford such distractions. Not then.

Perhaps after I recovered the gem, I could taste the Apple—if she'd let me, which was doubtful, not after she discovered the part I had for her to play in my little pageant at the earl's estate. But I couldn't worry about any of that. I had to keep my mind sharp and focused for the task that lay before me.

I took another deep breath. The sapphire was more important than kissing some infuriating chit, anyway.

She'd truly angered me that morning with her shallow contempt of Constance and the other ladies of The Birdhouse, and I'd still be angry if she hadn't told me what she'd done for the Brown girl.

Blasted woman! How could I be angry with her after she'd done a thing like that?

Devilish woman! One moment, I wanted to toss her into the river, and the next, I wanted to kiss her.

Deuced woman! I settled for walking sedately beside her and wondering if she'd ever let me kiss her.

She was trouble. Too damned attractive, and too damned intelligent. It wasn't that I was afraid of her discovering my secrets. I'd grown up on the streets of London, after all, and I knew how to cover my tracks. It would take an open frontal assault to batter down my defenses, and females were too delicate for that.

Not this one, my mind whispered. *This one is sturdy, tenacious, and stubborn as hell.* She'd never even heard the word "delicate."

She bent to pick a sheaf of delicate pink wildflowers, as though mocking my thoughts. "So . . . how do you fit in?" she asked.

"Beg pardon?"

"Why are you such a favorite here? The Blackthorn villagers all treat you as a patron saint. And you appear to be the darling of The Birdhouse, too—though it is clear you have never . . . conducted any business transactions with them. How did you come to be their pet? What is your part in their story?"

Evidently, she'd never heard the word "delicacy," either.

We turned into Birdhouse Lane, and the kitchen chimneys were just visible over the tops of the chestnut trees. I made a show of inhaling deeply. "Ah! Fresh bread," I exclaimed. "Is there a more delicious aroma in all the world?"

"You are changing the subject."

"You're right."

"You are a gem," she said facetiously.

"So are you."

"A diamond of the foulest water?"

I laughed. "The most fetid, stinking, tainted water there is." I opened the front door of The Birdhouse and sketched a bow as she entered, confident I'd dodged a bullet by changing the subject, but just before she cleared the door, she stopped to look me in the eye.

"I will not stop, you know. I shall ferret out your past in time."

I had no time to reply before a trio of Birds—Hope, Jane, and Penelope—swooped down and ushered her upstairs, chattering something about a portrait. As I stood there watching them ascend arm-in-arm, with Apple smiling the while, I suddenly realized what a good actress she was. By her own admission, The Birdhouse challenged her moral sensibilities, but Apple hadn't betrayed any discomfort at all. She seemed as at ease at The Birdhouse as she did back at The Dancing Maiden, where she was as quick to speak with traveling Gypsies as she was with the rare Quality who passed through. She kept her private opinions private, and her courtesy public.

A thief such as I is no stranger to the *ton*. I'd met or observed more than my share of titled ladies in my travels. Apple wasn't a peeress or even a member of the gentry, and yet she behaved as well as any tonnish lady I'd ever had the pleasure—or displeasure—of knowing.

Finding myself alone for the moment, I looked into the garden and was unsurprised to discover Mr. Bird strolling the roses with Constance. I frowned at his gait. He was limping even more now than he had been earlier. Even from this distance, I could see that his knuckles were a little knobby, and I fancied it vexed him to be growing frail. He was a thief, after all, and I knew how I would feel in his situation.

CHAPTER SIX

Affected simplicity is a subtle imposture.
      —François, Duc De La Rochefoucauld

I do not know what I'd expected when I realized The Birdhouse was a brothel, but it was not kindness and gentility.

Dinner that night was superb. The ladies' gowns were elegant, their manners refined. Miss Cherry sat at the head of the table with Uncle John and me in places of honor to her left and right. Posthumous sat at the far end of the table smiling benevolently, and as dinner wore on, I realized that none of the birds had ever shared a nest with him. He treated them almost as beloved aunts and sisters, rather than as lovers.

I told myself I did not care. It did not matter to me what his relationship was to the inhabitants of The Birdhouse. I was not interested in *nesting* with Mr. Jones! Still, I found myself more at ease than I had since I arrived, and was actually enjoying myself just a little.

Halfway through dinner, Mr. Jones told the company about what I'd done for Sarah Brown.

"Why, what a lovely thing for you to do," Jane said.

"Yes, lovely," Hope murmured, "but . . ." She bit her lip.

"Ah." Miss Cherry nodded. "Yes. Yes, I see."

"Is something amiss?" I asked.

Hope looked pained. "What about the other children?"

"Mmm," Jane intoned, "she is right. The other children's costumes are not likely to be much better than Sarah's mermaid. And now Sarah's lovely angel costume will make the others look that much worse."

An older lady named Beatrice tapped the table for their attention. "We could help the children with their costumes. We have yards and yards of scrap fabric and idle hands."

They all burst out talking at once. "Could we, Miss Cherry?" "Do you think they would accept our help?" "Could we attend the pageant?" "I have some lamb's wool that would be perfect for the three kings' beards!"

Miss Cherry gave her consent to the plan and said she would make inquiries in the village, and the ladies were chattering happily about helping the children with their costumes when the commotion broke out.

It began with the doorbell ringing. Miss Cherry started, and her wide eyes sought Mr. Jones's. The ladies froze, their forks poised in midair. Clearly, visitors were not expected.

Loud voices erupted in the front hall and gave way to angry shouting as the visitors barged past the footman and into the house.

"Where're they?" an inebriated voice slurred.

Calmly, Mr. Jones folded his napkin and stood up.

Miss Cherry said softly, "Careful, *mon cher.*"

Mr. Jones had no time to reply before two large, well-dressed but disheveled men staggered into the dining room. "Look a' that Johnson, we're just in time for dessert!"

The other man fastened his eyes on Jane and licked his lips.

Miss Cherry cleared her throat. "The Birdhouse is not receiving guests today, gentlemen. Kindly return another time—perhaps when you are not foxed," she said pointedly.

Mr. Johnson hooked his thumb at Posthumous Jones. "What about him?"

"And him," his friend said, nodding toward Uncle John. "I'll wager they ain't *family.*" Both men laughed raucously at the cruel joke, and I watched Mr. Jones's body tense in preparation for a fight.

Now, I ran a tight ship at The Dancing Maiden, but over the years, inevitably, I had witnessed my share of brawls. I recognized that a fight in The Birdhouse's crowded dining room, with all its glass and wine and candles, would be very dangerous, and Mr. Jones was no match for two drunken bruisers. Uncle John saw it too and, standing up, rounded the table to stand beside Posthumous Jones. Looking wildly about for something—anything!— to use as a weapon, my eyes fixed upon a heavy candlestick standing on the table in front of me. But my fingers had barely touched it when Miss Cherry laid her hand over mine.

"Not to worry," she whispered. "Just watch."

Mr. Jones took a step forward. "You'll find The King's Breath down in the village a fine establishment. Good ale. Tell the ostler's daughter I sent you and to put a round on my tab." He took another step forward.

Mr. Johnson turned red and, reaching out with one meaty hand, he roughly took possession of Jane's milky shoulder. "Here now, we ain't going anywhere 'til we've had our dessert!"

Mr. Jones shook his head and sighed. "Wrong answer."

Five seconds later, both men lay on the floor, whimpering.

Grasping the edge of the tablecloth on the sideboard, Mr. Jones had given it a swift jerk, leaving all the dishes in place. Winding it around his fists, he'd danced behind the men, looped the cloth about their necks, and given a savage yank. Their heads smashed together with a resounding crack, and they slumped to the floor, Mr. Jones making use of the slack in the tablecloth to create a noose of sorts. He cinched it down with his heel, and they were at his mercy, and they knew it.

"Please!" Mr. Johnson squealed. "Let me go!"

"I *will* let you go," Mr. Jones said, "the second I throw you out the door."

"We'll go!" the other man said. "We didn't mean no harm!"

"Oh, Pos," Jane said, "You aren't going to hurt them, are you? They have visited us before, and they were perfect gentlemen. They're only foxed is all."

Several of the ladies murmured an agreement, and Mr. Jones looked to Miss Cherry for confirmation. She held his gaze for a moment and then nodded.

Mr. Jones let go. "On your way, gentlemen." He followed them out of the dining room and down the long hall.

As Uncle John sat back down, I stood up. "Where are you going?" he asked.

"I confess I do not feel quite as charitable as the rest of the ladies present. I find I have the desire to see those two gentlemen shown the door." I smiled. "I am hoping Mr. Jones is at least a little rough."

Penelope stood up. "I will come too."

"Stay, my dear," Miss Cherry said. "You have not finished your dinner."

No one mentioned the half slice of pie sitting at my place, and I moved off after Posthumous Jones and the intruders. Passing down the hall, I came upon the still form of Callahan, the footman who had been on watch at the front door. He was out cold and already had a nasty bruise on his cheekbone. As I bent to feel for a pulse, he came to and scrambled to his feet, embarrassed but not permanently damaged, and I hurried after Mr. Jones once more.

I came into the front hall just in time to hear Mr. Jones say in a steely, yet quiet, voice, "If I ever find that you have come here and behaved badly again . . . if you have so much as a drop to drink, either before or while you are here . . . I will kill you, understand?"

Both men's throats bobbed as they swallowed hard, and they nodded, apparently convinced.

"The King's Breath is that way." He pointed, and the unsteady men somehow managed to mount their horses and ride off into the night.

He stood there watching a few moments to see that they did not come back, and I stood there watching him. I couldn't help feeling a little feminine thrill of admiration for what he'd done. He'd moved so quickly and with such sure action! He was a man with whom any woman could feel safe and protected.

A man like that would be useful around The Dancing Maiden.

As the seconds passed, his tense body relaxed. Finally, he sighed and sagged against the doorframe.

"Would you really kill them?" I asked.

He didn't move, didn't look up, thinking for a moment before he answered quietly, "I would kill to protect any woman."

And he could do it, too. I'd underestimated him. It seemed I'd been doing a lot of that lately.

"I apologize," I said, and he turned to me.

"For what?"

I walked to stand beside him. "The ladies of The Birdhouse are just that—ladies. I should know better than to judge people before I come to know them."

He sank to a pink damask sofa and rubbed the back of his neck. "What changed your mind about them?"

"They did. Did you see their faces light up when Miss Beatrice suggested that they help the children with their costumes?"

"I did."

"And they were ready to forgive those two"—I nodded into the night—"where I, frankly, wanted blood."

He smiled. "I saw your hand on the candlestick."

I sat next to him. "I am sorry. I should have trusted you."

"You did not know you could. I admire your quick thinking and your courage." He brushed his fingers across my elbow. "You and Mr. Bird are cut from the same cloth."

I sighed. "Not quite. Uncle John did not behave as a barbarian upon arrival. He took the ladies of The Birdhouse for the modest, kind, and gentle creatures they are. I have been secretly looking down on them, while they have been nothing but warm to me since I arrived. Do you know they took me upstairs when we returned from the village today to sketch my portrait? They said they wanted something to remember me by!"

"You sound surprised."

"I was," I admitted, "but no longer. Whoever made up the phrase 'no better then she ought to be' did not have *these* ladies in mind." I shrugged and shook my head. "I cannot help liking them."

"Nor should you try," he said. "Come, let us return to dinner."

The rest of that evening and the next day passed all too quickly. Admiral Termagant's navy returned the next morning to fit my new clothes. The seamstresses had been working all day and through the night to finish, and they all wore dark circles under their eyes. After my fitting, they retired to the sunny parlor to finish the garments they'd fashioned, and Hope, Jane, and I served the tired seamstresses tea and sandwiches at midday. Most of them had appeared uncomfortable when first they arrived, but all smiled and murmured their sincere thanks when we served them, grateful to put down their needles for a moment and to eat.

It was then that I realized I was no longer uncomfortable at The Birdhouse. My welcome had been nothing but warm, and the ladies of The Birdhouse were, without exception, polite, gracious, intelligent, amiable, and attentive. I'd been accepted as part of the household, it seemed, even though I wasn't truly one of them.

After luncheon, we left the seamstresses to their toil and everyone at The Birdhouse, both residents and guests, ventured outside to picnic and collect the late dewberries that grew in the shady dell near the ice house. The grass was luxuriant and green, the air was cool, and the birds slid merrily across the sky as though it were blue ice, singing and scolding, and seeming to have as grand a time as we were having on the ground. Riddles and jests flew almost as fast, and for the first time since I do not know when, I found myself relaxing, slowing down inside. There were no menus to plan, no laundry to oversee, no accounts to balance. I could have stayed right there picking dewberries the rest of my life and been perfectly happy.

It was there I learned what Mr. Jones had been doing in the village morning last. He was berry-picking alongside me when . . .

. . . when her uncle approached us, smiling and holding out a nearly full pail. He looked over his shoulder at Constance, who was standing off a little way, before saying in a near-whisper, "Thank you, dearling, for that little present you left in my room yesterday."

"Present?" Apple asked.

"Oh, yes! This much weight would have hurt my hand yesterday," he told her, lifting his pail. "My rheumatism is much improved."

"I am glad, Uncle," Apple said, "but I don't—"

"And—bless me!—I slept like a babe in arms last night! Do you think you could find me another bottle before we leave?"

She glanced up at me. Obviously, she'd seen me with the bottle in the village yesterday. "Certainly, Uncle," she said. "I will do my best."

"Good," Mr. Bird said with a nod. "Fine!" He gave her a pat on the head and strode off toward Constance, looking spry indeed.

Apple turned to me. "Laudanum, I presume?"

I nodded. "That's right. Why didn't you tell him it was me who brought it for him?"

"You did not want me to," she said. "'Rheumatism comes and goes,'" she quoted me, "'but if you take away a man's dignity, it is gone forever.'"

"Clever girl. Good, kind, clever girl! You're learning."

As she acknowledged the praise with a sedate nod of the head, a traitor dimple appeared in her cheek, but then she frowned. "How much do I owe you?"

"Twenty guineas."

"*Twenty guineas?*" she cried. "For laudanum?"

"No, Apple, for the compliment I just paid you. The laudanum was free. Oh, I see now!" I feigned sudden understanding. "You meant how much laudanum should your uncle take! Five drops in his tea at night and three in the morning, the doctor said."

"You knew very well what I meant—and procuring the laudanum for Uncle was very kind of you. And now *you* owe *me* twenty guineas for the compliment I just paid you, so we are even."

"Shh . . ." I held my finger to my lips. "You will spoil my reputation."

"Too late," she said, "everyone here seems to like you."

"Except you," I said, popping a dewberry into my mouth and eyeing her comically.

She pasted on a serious expression. "Indeed not."

"You do not like me."

"No," she said, "I do not believe I do."

"No," I said, "you do not like me, you *love* me! You want to *ravish* me!" I sat on the ground and patted my lap.

She gave a bark of laughter. "You are mad!" she cried and skipped away, a chuckle dancing in the air behind her.

I *was* mad—mad with a desire to kiss her! I stared after her shaking my head.

Apple was a different person since she'd come here. Or was it I who had changed? Had our mere prolonged proximity been the cause of my increased desire? Or was it something else?

I'd never seen her smile so much. She was irresistible there in the sunshine, with the wind blowing through her dark hair, her cheeks full of roses, and her eyes full of sparkling light!

And things didn't improve when we returned to the house, for the ladies immediately herded her into her chamber, where they bade her don a new gown, a rose-colored concoction that made my heart constrict when I saw her float down the stairs in it. She was stunning, and she knew it. She wore a smile that bespoke confidence. Not just confidence as an innkeeper, a cook, or a servant, but as a woman. A lovely woman who knew I wanted her, by Jove!

It was all I could do not to carry her back up those stairs to my bedchamber. I wanted to touch her, taste her, smell her! I wanted to bury my hands in her dark hair and spread it across my pillow. I wanted to kiss her until she was gasping for more.

Hell and blast, I was shaking with desire!

Shocked and disturbed at the sudden force of my reaction, I turned away. "You will do."

The young ladies gasped. "Beast!" said one. "Jerk!" cried another. "What a crock," said a third.

Erma shook her head. "He wasn't any of those, my dears. If I never teach you anything else, you must learn this: men are fragile. Pos wasn't trying to be mean; he was protecting his heart. Like throwing your hands up to protect your face when someone throws a ball. It was an instinctive reaction, not something he thought about at all. But don't worry. You'll see. He comes to regret what he said . . ."

* * *

I was hurt.

Hurt? La, I was crushed! I had never in my whole life been turned out so well. The sunrise-colored gown swaying with a silken rustle, the soft white gloves caressing my hands, the simple ribbon winding through my upswept hair—all were far better than I'd ever thought to own. I thought I looked a little beautiful. I knew I looked far different than I had an hour before, and that I'd never do better.

That moment was the pinnacle of my life's loveliness.

And so, when he turned away without a second glance, I was crushed. But as I stood there in near shock, several of the ladies traded speaking glances, and those who did not wore half-smiles. Miss Cherry smiled openly and winked at me, and I realized with a start that they all believed Posthumous Jones was only feigning his indifference!

I felt my face flush. I am certain it was pinker than my gown for at least the next hour. He pretended to ignore that, too, which sent the ladies into paroxysms of imprisoned laughter several times. They had to quit the room or turn away, suddenly interested in the hems of their gowns or in a painting or vase.

Unfortunately, the mirthful mood didn't last.

It was our last day at The Birdhouse, and the later it got, the more subdued the atmosphere. Dinner that night wasn't the pleasant occasion it had been the previous nights. Uncle John was uncharacteristically glum, the ladies were quieter than usual, and I said almost nothing. Only Mr. Jones and Miss Cherry seemed unaffected by the prospect of our parting early on the morrow.

After a short evening of music in the parlor, we thanked them all and said our goodbyes so we could turn in early.

"I will come back soon," I heard Uncle say.

"How lovely," Miss Cherry said with a smile as though this were the first she'd heard of it—a circumstance I was certain wasn't true. "It is a shame you do not live closer. We have all enjoyed your company. Please feel free to return whenever you wish. We would all be so glad to welcome you again."

"Thank you, Miss Cherry. I would like that very much," I said sincerely, "but I cannot. I have The Dancing Maiden, you see, and—"

"Say no more, *cherie!*" Constance laughed. "I know what a burden commerce can be!"

We all laughed at that, and there was no embarrassment in it for any of us, I fancied. I know there was none in my own heart. "Oh . . . I do like you," I said. "And I like this place."

"I like it here," Uncle said. "In fact, I like it here so much I am thinking of moving here."

"Really!" Miss Cherry cried. "How perfectly lovely!"

Uncle? Move away from The Dancing Maiden? The idea was shocking, to be sure, but much to my own surprise, I could not muster any degree of disapproval. He'd fallen arse over instep in love with Miss Constance Cherry. Any fool could see that. And Miss Cherry certainly wasn't doing anything to discourage his attention. And why should she? We none of us were surrounded by dukes and princesses. The Birdhouse was populated by prostitutes and their paramours, while at The Dancing Maiden, we were surrounded by riff-raff. La, as far as so-called Good Society was concerned, we were *all* riff-raff! None of our friends would care one whit if Mr. Bird married his lady lovebird.

Bidding everyone goodnight, I climbed the stairs. It wasn't until then I stopped to think that Posthumous Jones was a possible exception. He had an invitation to an earl's house party, after all, and a man who walked around with huge gems in his pockets was sure to have other lofty friends. I wondered how they reacted to his association with The Birdhouse. But then Mr. Jones was probably just as secretive with them about The Birdhouse as he'd been with me. He'd dodged the question of how he'd come to be treated as a member of The Birdhouse family rather than as a paying guest.

I tried to put the matter from my mind. Since it clearly
made no difference to Uncle or Constance, it was none
of my concern. All I cared about was that the happy pair
enjoyed each other's company. Their age gave them
much in common. And it wasn't as though either of
them were hasty or impulsive where their hearts were concerned. Neither of them were young and neither had ever
married. How lovely that they had both found love at last!
I would encourage Uncle to move forthwith. I would be
alone at The Dancing Maiden, and I would miss him
dreadfully, but Blackthorn Village was only a day's drive
away, and they could visit whenever they wished.

I almost floated to my chamber and laughed more
than once on the way. And yet, in spite of Uncle's good
fortune, the swallows on my ceiling seemed sadder that
night, the clouds painted there a little darker. We were
leaving tomorrow, and a maid had already packed my
things and laid out my traveling clothes for the morning.
I had nothing to do but wash and get into bed, but I didn't
fall asleep until the small hours. Instead, I lay there
musing upon how quickly I had come to revere a house
full of *demimondaine!*

CHAPTER SEVEN

In a blush, love finds a barrier.

—Virgil

Early the next morning, we took a hasty breakfast and then assembled at the front of the house. The sky was still dark, and the lamps on the coach were lit. Mist clung to the ground and everything was wet with dew. Most of the ladies were still asleep at that hour, but Miss Cherry had arisen to see us off—or so I thought.

Stepping down from the front door carrying a large bag, she stepped lightly over to the coach just as Mr. Jones was handing me inside.

"I am coming with you," she announced.

"You are?" Uncle crowed. "Splendid!" He patted Miss Cherry's hand and climbed aboard the coach after her. "Glad to hear it, my dear. But I am tired. Up too late last night. I am for bed." With that, he sat next to her, sagged against the side of the coach, laid his head against the window, and appeared to sink instantly to sleep.

I looked toward Mr. Jones for confirmation of Miss Cherry's assertion that she was coming along.

"Miss Cherry is familiar with my culinary requirements," he said, "She will supervise you."

Miss Cherry laughed a little too gaily as he settled himself on the seat next to me. "I would have offered to cook for him," she said, "but Mr. Jones has no wish to be poisoned." She fussed with her traveling costume, avoiding my eyes as she had at last night's dinner—a dinner at which she and Mr. Jones were the only animated diners.

"You both knew about this last night. Why did you not tell the rest of us?"

Mr. Jones shrugged. "We were still unsure."

Rubbish! They had deliberately hid it from me, and I wanted to know why, so I dug a little deeper. "It seems odd to me, a gentleman traveling with three servants, two women and a man."

"Miss Grey," Mr. Jones said, tiredly giving the impression we'd been debating the matter for hours, "you are hardly in a position to know how a gentleman travels. Your little inn doesn't see much *tonnish* traffic."

I bristled, for I had the sudden impression that what seemed on the outside to be a bland statement had been meant as an insult.

"Am I meant to take offence?" I asked.

"You are meant only to take my orders," he responded with a shrug and then looked out the window. It was a clear dismissal, and I resolved to be angry with him. Again.

And then my anger evaporated into shock, for I realized with sudden clarity that he was hiding something. Lying!

Why?

I had no idea. And, I could hardly ask him. He was as close-lipped as he'd always been. I'd been in his company for three days and still didn't know his real name with any certainty. La, I'd been such a ninny to relax around him! I couldn't believe anything Mr. Posthumous Jack Jones Morgan said.

At that moment, as fate would have it, another piece

of the puzzle fell into place. Or, more correctly, out of Mr.
Jones's pocket and onto the floor. A coin.

He often fiddled with coins in an absent fashion. And
I'd seen him amuse the village children with them back
in Lower Ridington. He would make a coin disappear and
then find it again in a giggling child's nose or ear.

But as this coin rolled onto the floor and he reached
for it, I realized it wasn't a coin at all—and that I'd seen
one like it before. It was identical to the little gold medallion Sarah Brown had been wearing around her neck, the
one she'd said Miss Cherry gave to all of the birds who
flew her nest.

And then I understood.

Posthumous Jones's mother had been one of Miss
Cherry's birds! And that business about changing his
name and Miss Cherry helping to conceal his identity was
about his parentage.

I nearly wept in relief, for a suspicion had crept insid-
iously into my mind, and I'd begun to wonder if Mr.
Jones had something terrible to hide. I wanted to tell him
that now and to hear him laugh. I wanted to reassure him
that I didn't care about his origin. It didn't matter to me
what his mother had done or that he didn't know who his
father was.

I wanted to tell him I was glad he wasn't the son of some
blasted duke, for I was beginning to . . . well, to have feelings for him.

He was intelligent and kind and . . . and, as difficult as
it was at first to believe of a man who spent his spare time
in a brothel, he was a gentleman. I kept thinking of the
amazing way he had thrown those two men out of The Birdhouse and of the quiet intensity in his voice when he said
he would kill to protect a woman. I felt safe with him.

But I couldn't tell him any of that. How could I?

So . . . I hear your mother was a prostitute.

or

La! I do not give a fig about your unfortunate upbringing!

or, as his name was Posthumous, perhaps

My, it just occurred to me that your name might be a ruse to cover for the fact that you don't have the first notion who your father was!

Uh . . . no. Utterly impossible. So I sat nearly silent until noon, when we took our midday meal and let our horses rest at a small inn a few villages away.

Miss Cherry was still eating when Mr. Jones rose from the rough table. She was a slow and dainty eater, a woman of the aristocracy who'd grown up with five-hour suppers. Uncle was a fast eater, except when he was dining with Miss Cherry. I'd have wagered my last farthing he would take his last bite within seconds of hers. When Mr. Jones excused himself, I followed.

"I hope your uncle and Constance do not mind our absence too much," he said, emerging into the sunshine.

I smiled. "I doubt they have noticed we are gone."

He laughed and paused at the entrance to the stable-yard. "I am going to check on the coach and horses."

"There is a coachman for that."

"I prefer to oversee the horses myself. A single lame foot would cost us at least a day's drive, and it is crucial that I not miss a moment of the house party."

"Oh? Hmm! Will there perhaps be a lady awaiting the pleasure of your company there?"

"Jealous?"

"No," I lied.

"Good, because there will be several."

"Liar."

"Jealous."

I laughed. "I am not!"

"You are because you *love* me."

"I do not!"

"You want to *ravish* me!"

"*Shhh!*" I hissed. "We are in the middle of a stableyard!"

He laughed again. "Come on, Apple. You can keep me company while I check on the horses. You can entertain yourself watching my manly musculature or some such rot."

"Talk about rot. If I come to the stables, it will be to help."

"That won't be necessary."

"Mr. Jones, I do know my way around the stables. I am an innkeeper."

"Yes," he said, "but *today* you look like a lady."

I laughed. "Should I think that flattery or an insult?"

His eyes took a leisurely trip up and down my smart gray traveling costume, and I felt myself blush. "What do you think, Apple?"

"I think you are an incorrigible rake."

He grinned. "Quite right. Do not forget it."

"Do I have a choice?"

"Not if I can help it." And to prove his point, he took a bright red apple from his pocket, took a large bite, and smacked his lips. "Mmm!"

I accompanied him to the stable even though I had nothing to do there. Wasting no time, he leaned against the flank of one of The Birdhouse's fine blacks, picked up the animal's hoof, and ran an expert hand down its leg, feeling for heat or swelling before checking for stones. He knew what he was doing.

"You are as capable with the horses as you are with everything else. What do you do? Your occupation, I mean. Are you employed?"

He glanced up at me. "I used to be."

"But not anymore?"

"My, but you are curious this morning, Apple. No, not anymore. I invested wisely."

"Then you are a gentleman of sorts."

"Of sorts," he repeated with an amused lift of one black eyebrow.

I laughed. "Of the best sort. Honestly, I had begun to think, Mr. Jones, that you had some nefarious past."

"As?"

"As a smuggler, a runaway indenture . . . a debtor, perhaps."

"Or a thief?"

"La, no!" I scoffed. "You are no thief."

He put down one hoof and lifted the next. "And how do you know that?"

"You are absurd."

"I am serious." He felt the leg while regarding me thoughtfully. "I spend my spare time in a brothel, dress in workingman's clothes, lay claim to more than one name, and carry jewels worth a king's ransom in my pocket. How do you know I did not steal the sapphire from someone?"

"Thieves are evil, and you are not," I said.

"I see. So, automatically, I am some rich cit?"

"You *are* en route to an earl's house party," I pointed out.

He opened his mouth to reply, but at that moment a smart, black-lacquered carriage rolled into the stable-yard with a clatter, and I scooted out of the way. A liveried footman jumped to the ground, took down the carriage's step, and opened the door with a flourish.

Out of the carriage stepped a nightmare.

CHAPTER EIGHT

Love looks not with the eyes, but with the mind.
—William Shakespeare

Miss Grey skittered behind the black, but she needn't have bothered. The man who stepped down from the carriage didn't so much as glance in our direction.

Dressed in a heavily embroidered pink striped waistcoat and bottle green jacket, he was the epitome of a tulip, a tonnish dandy who concerned himself with nothing more than presenting a fashionable image. The stables were beneath his notice, and he hadn't seen my little Apple. He was too busy sneering in the direction of the little inn.

"Is this it?" He lifted a lace-edged handkerchief to his nose.

"I am sorry, sir," his coachman said, "but it's this place or none. The horses can't go no further, not if you want 'em to make it all the way."

I looked at the poor, tired beasts and tensed. Their mouths were flecked with foam, their flanks caked with dried sweat, and their eyes were dull.

The dandy heaved a dramatic sigh and marched into the inn without another word to his driver and footman, who exchanged conspiratorial acid glances and then moved to unhitch the horses, patting necks and speaking softly.

I turned to Apple. "Who was that?"

She picked at her sleeve. "Who?"

"The cretin who has you looking like you've seen a ghost. Do not pretend for a moment that you do not know him. I have been lied to by the best, and you aren't even close."

She closed her eyes for a moment and sighed. "Portman Lowell." She rubbed her forehead and groaned, and instantly I wanted to pummel Mr. Lowell for that.

"And?" I prompted, deciding I'd better learn more about Mr. Lowell before I gave him a black eye or two.

A little color returned to her face. "He courted me furiously until I was seventeen—not that I wanted any part of him. He made my skin crawl. Still does." I shuddered. "So now my secret is out," I said, trying to muster a smile. "I am a coward, afraid of mincing, kiss-stealing tulips."

"Apple, the man makes *my* skin crawl, and he has never tried to kiss me!"

I exhaled and gave a little laugh.

"What happened between you?"

"Nothing, thank goodness! A distant cousin of his died unexpectedly and without an heir. Mr. Lowell had wanted The Dancing Maiden—"

"And you, I presume?"

I nodded, my lip curling. "Of that there can be no doubt. But after his inheritance, he told all the countryside that *I'd* been the one chasing *him*—and that I was even more beneath his notice than I had been before. He said he was now a member of a peer's household and he admonished that it was beyond an innkeeper's social capacity to speak to the likes of him. 'You are hardly more than a servant.' I think those were his exact words. And now . . ." Her voice trailed off, and she shrugged.

"And now you are a servant?"

She looked down at her hands. "I do not regret agree-ing to serve you, sir. It was good of you to offer to keep me out of trouble, and—and Mr. Lowell is right. An innkeeper is hardly more than a servant, and he is rich and—"

"And a fool," I said, with more vehemence than I in-tended, judging by her widened eyes and open mouth. I shook my head and rolled my eyes skyward. "I am sorry. I do not know your Mr. Lowell, of course, but—"

"He is not *my* Mr. Lowell!"

"—but any man who casts a lovely, intelligent woman aside for money is a fool indeed."

She looked down at her hands. "Thank you," she said quietly.

"For calling Mr. Lowell a fool?" I teased. "Or for lying and saying you are lovely and intelligent?"

"Both," she said with a wide grin, laughed, and walked to the inn. She obviously didn't believe I'd been lying.

I was still trying to convince myself I *had* been lying when she tossed over her shoulder, "If I see Mr. Lowell, I think I will embrace him and announce that I have fleas!"

I laughed in spite of myself, watching the sway of her hips beneath the gray traveling gown she wore, and then with a supreme force of will I closed my eyes. *I say, old boy, you cannot afford this distraction!*

I quit the stable and made for the well, where I doused my face in cold water and tried to think of the sapphire, but I couldn't keep thoughts of her buried, down where they belonged.

"I'll bet that's not all that wouldn't stay down!"

Erma gave her a stern look. "Tamara! For shame!"

The young woman looked crestfallen. "I'm sorry, ma'am."

"How many times must you be told?" Erma admonished

her. "It's a wager, not a bet! Now, where was I?" Shrieks
of laughter erupted at her feet, but Erma read on, un-
perturbed, and her charges quieted, hanging onto each
juicy syllable.

Mr. Stinky—the name I'd given Portman Lowell when
we were but children—had evidently demanded and received quick service and was tucked up in his room by the
time I stepped into the inn's small common room, so I
did not get the chance to torment him.

Mr. Jones took care of that for me the next morning.

We had just finished our breakfast and settled the bill
when Mr. Lowell minced and lisped his fashionable way
down the stairs. Taking Uncle John's arm, I whirled us
both around so that Mr. Lowell would not recognize us.

"Quite right, my dear!" Uncle whispered. "Insufferable pup! I am for the carriage!" With that, he drew Miss
Cherry outside.

Glancing up at Mr. Jones, I almost gasped, for he was
staring at Mr. Lowell with a malice so intense it made me
uncomfortable to look at him, and then suddenly his expression changed, softening with a hint of . . . what?
Amusement? Satisfied derision?

Instantly, I knew he was thinking of visiting some sort
of revenge upon Mr. Lowell!

"Mr. Jones!" I hissed.

"What?" He gave me a sidelong, innocent look.

"What are you thinking?"

"Nothing much," he replied with a shrug, "but just in
case, be ready to go along with whatever I say."

"What are you going to—"

He silenced me with a wink and, tucking my arm through
his, he strolled indolently toward the front door, where he
just stopped, deliberately blocking Mr. Lowell's egress. A few
seconds passed, and I could hear Mr. Lowell puffing with
impatience behind us.

"I say, my good man," he said. "I have a very important engagement to attend. Do step aside."

"I say, my dear Eve," said Mr. Jones. "I have a very impatient fly buzzing in my ear. Do you hear it?"

"Step aside, woman," Mr. Lowell cried, "and let your husband through the door! And by all things holy," he muttered, "eat less!"

I flinched. It wasn't that I wasted much time fretting about my slighty-too-generous proportions, and I didn't give a fig about Mr. Stinky's opinion—but I couldn't help the sudden stabbing notion that *Mr. Jones* might not like my curves.

La, Leah, get hold of yourself!

Mr. Jones wasn't quite a diamond of the first water, either. Right? So what if he was a mysteriously attractive, startlingly intelligent man? So what if I'd kissed him in my daydreams more than once or twice these past few days? I was nothing more than a momentary flirtation to him. That's all I ever had been, and that's all I ever would be. A stay at Chateau le Messr. Jones was a pleasant enough daydream, but I wouldn't want to live there!

And then, the dratted, confusing, infuriating, dear man changed my mind yet again.

He turned suddenly, taking me with him, and I found myself facing Mr. Lowell, who was too busy glaring at Mr. Jones to look at my face. I tried to be invisible while Mr. Lowell puffed up like an adder and sputtered, "I do not have all day to stand around waiting for—"

"We have not been introduced," Mr. Jones said evenly. "I am Fitzroy Noland, the Viscount Turnbull, and this"— he turned to me—"is my lady fair."

I nearly fell over.

Mr. Lowell, for his part, grew a sudden, simpering, adoring, sickeningly sweet smile on his weasel-like face and opened his mouth to speak but froze with his mouth open as he glanced down at me. His eyes bugged and then narrowed as they assessed my traveling costume, an elegant confection of the latest style fashioned of smooth, sea-green linen with rich blue satin trim.

I stifled a laugh, half glee, half nervous bubble.

He'd never seen me wearing anything so grand, and my hair was perfectly dressed. With such incongruous finery, a false name, seven years between then and now, and an imposing man at my side, would Mr. Stinky recognize me? I held my breath.

Remembering to close his mouth, he smiled nervously, glanced at Mr. Jones and then back to me. "Have we met?" he asked at last.

"Doubtful," Mr. Jones answered for me with a haughty chuckle that suggested the very idea was laughable. "My sweet travels in lofty—and very fast—circles." He patted my hand with apparent fondness. "I have always wondered what it would be like to tame a rakehell heiress," he said.

I laughed woodenly at his absurd witticism and wondered if I would collapse into a delicate, feminine heap when I fainted or if my rounded behind would bounce me into an undignified sprawl instead. Mr. Stinky was not stupid, and he certainly understood he'd been put in his place. I was sure he was going to bluster, scowl, and make a scene but instead, to my complete surprise, he gave a tight bow, said, "Good day to you," and beat a hasty exit.

Mr. Jones dropped my hand. "Does he blanch that white, or does the cave he crawled out of get no sunlight at all?"

I laughed so hard I nearly wept. "Oh! I haven't seen anything that comical in years! Did you see the way his mouth worked? He looked like a fish out of water, and I am so grateful, but—oh Pos!—an heiress?"

"Think he believed me?" Mr. Jones asked with a grin.

"What possessed you?"

He shrugged. "I wanted to deflate the puffed-up popinjay. It irritated me how he spoke to you."

"But I am not really your 'lady fair,'" I said, "so there was no need for your pride to be hurt."

"It wasn't my pride that was challenged, but your honor. No lady should have to suffer such clods. He needed to be put in his place." He stepped closer. "And speaking of places"—he glanced around the common room—"this place appears empty."

I looked around. He was right. "The innkeeper's wife was here a moment"—he took my hand and pulled me close—"ago!" I squeaked and looked up to discover his eyes focused upon my mouth! I moistened my lips, which seemed to have grown to the size of twin elephants. "We are alone," I said. "This is not proper. We might be doing anything in here!"

"Exactly," he said, taking a step closer.

"We should be going."

He nodded and leaned even closer. "We should."

He leaned closer still, his sky-blue eyes flicked down to my mouth, time slowed down, and I was suddenly aware that he meant to kiss me.

"Are you aware," he murmured, "that you called me 'Pos' just now?"

I managed a minute shake of my head. I could feel his breath on my lips as we both tilted our heads—and a voice rang out behind us.

"Upon my honor!"

We both deloped, of course.

The speaker, a portly man in his forties, bustled up to us and pumped Mr. Jones's hand enthusiastically. "It *is* you! Mrs. Cunningham fetched me—she's running down the street calling out your name." He pounded Mr. Jones on the back. "Well met, Mr. Stone! Well met! My, but it is an honor to see you again, sir! And who be this lovely lady?"

"Yes, *Mr. Stone*," I said, raising an eyebrow. "Do please introduce me to your friend."

Mr. Jones developed storm cloud brows over those fair-sky blue eyes of his, and he grasped me by the arm, turning me about none too gently. "I am sorry, Mr. Bentley, but we must away. Late, late!" he tossed over his shoulder as he hustled me out the door. Plowing across the stableyard toward the waiting coach, he uttered not one word. And neither did I.

Instead, I was desperately grappling for a reasonable, satisfying, *legal* explanation for Mr. Jones having not one but two false names.

CHAPTER NINE

*A sudden bold and unexpected question doth many times
surprise a man and lay him open.*

—Sir Francis Bacon

Apple said no more than a dozen words until midday
when we stopped to take luncheon and to rest the horses.
There was no inn, so we chose a likely tree at the crest of
a lonely hill, where I could keep watch, of course. The two
of us ate in near silence, with Constance and Mr. Bird
keeping up an almost steady stream of lively conversation.

It wasn't until after the meal when the elders took a turn
down the hill to stretch their legs in the company of the
coachman and footman that Apple finally questioned me,
as I'd known she would. I was prepared.

"Why do you need more than one false name?" she said
quietly, suddenly. She wasn't looking at me, and I knew
she suspected I had something bad to hide.

I shrugged with apparent unconcern. "It was something
foolish I did when I was a lad. I traveled everywhere, and
I gave myself a different name in every village, pretending
to be some sort of smuggler or highwayman or army hero
traveling in secret. As time passed, it just seemed easier to
keep it up than to tell everyone I met that I'd lied."

"Oh." Her shoulders drooped a little as the tension left them, and I knew she believed me. She stood and walked to the other side of the road, stretching her hands above her head and then rubbing the small of her back. "What do you mean you traveled?" she asked, turning to regard me with a look of frank curiosity.

"I was orphaned at eight. I was alone and had nowhere to go."

Her face folded into soft lines of sympathy. "I am sorry. I know how it feels to lose one's parents. It must have been even worse for you, though. At least I had a place to stay and Uncle to comfort me."

I began gathering the leavings of the meal.

She moved to help. "It was your mother who died when you were eight, then?"

I folded the heavy yellow quilt we'd all sat upon. "You are thinking of my name?"

"Posthumous." She nodded and, taking the quilt from me, she tucked it away in the coach's boot. "The name is reserved for boys whose fathers die before their births. I simply assumed—"

"Hallooo!" called Mr. Bird from thirty yards down the hill. The quartet was nearly back, and I was glad to have an excuse to veer from Apple's line of questioning. Walking down the hill, I offered my arm to Constance, and soon we were rolling down the road once more, framed by verdant hills brimming with ancient walls, gurgling brooks, and meadows full of late summer flowers.

Apple was back to her usual loquacity, chattering animatedly with her uncle and Constance on inane topics such as the view and the weather. And I relaxed, which was a foolish thing to do, for Apple wasn't stupid, and my explanation for my multiple names hadn't quite satisfied her, as I found out a few hours later.

It was late in the afternoon, and we were all tired. Mr. Bird was sagged against the side of the coach softly snoring, and

Constance was staring absently out the window when Apple spoke.

"Where did you and your mother live before she died?"

Constance's eyes opened a little wider, but she didn't move.

"London," I replied.

"Were you born there?"

I nodded.

"Was your mother born there, as well?"

"No. She was from the country."

"Near London?"

"West Sussex. Moved to London with her parents when she was quite small and never left."

I watched Apple glance toward Constance, who was studiously avoiding both the conversation and Apple's eyes. Indecision marched across the younger woman's features, and for a second I thought she would press further, but then she subsided and looked back out the window. Not that I could relax. She was too clever to allow even a slight inconsistency slip past her unchallenged.

I didn't know whether to be happy about that or not.

A few leagues slid by and the coachman gave a whistle, awakening Mr. Bird, and we all gazed out the window at our destination. Below us stretched a shallow green valley with a wide blue river shining at its bottom. Above, a massive gray stone house sat enthroned upon a gentle hillside, presiding over a tidy village that straddled a river a mile downstream.

I pointed toward the enormous house. "Our destination."

"William Maddermark, the Earl of Instep," Constance said on a sigh. "I have heard it whispered he really is mad."

"Love must be involved, then," Mr. Bird said, gazing fondly at Constance.

"He is unmarried," she returned.

"Unrequited love. It would make any man mad."

Constance smiled softly. "Not to worry, *mon cher*." She patted the old man's hand.

Apple and I shared a speaking glance. We both knew Constance wasn't talking about the earl.

As the coach rolled slowly down the valley, I knew I should be thinking about what I was going to say when we arrived, about the false gem in my pocket, about my plan for stealing its real counterpart. But all I could think of was what I'd said to Apple that morning back at the inn. She'd been "lovely" and "intelligent," "my lady fair."

What the devil had possessed me?

She was pretty and clever, and I quite plainly desired her, much to my occasional discomfort, but that business about her being my lady? Pure claptrap! At least that's what it ought to have been. And that's what I meant it as. Wasn't it?

It did not signify. She hadn't given the matter a second thought, I was sure.

Still, I'd seen her eyes as I'd leaned close to kiss her that morning. I'd watched them widen in surprise and then relax in surrender. I'd watched her pupils flare with desire. We'd always had an easy if somewhat distant friendship, but our proximity over the past few days had fostered deeper feelings within both of us. Desire in me and, unless my mark went wide, tenderness in her.

Hers were feelings I was unprepared to reciprocate and follow down their natural path. I hadn't been lying that morning. I did think she was lovely and intelligent, a lady fair. But she was not *my* lady fair, and after this misadventure, she never would be. I'd missed my chance at kissing her. Whatever tender feelings she had for me would evaporate as soon as we arrived at the earl's estate.

That thought had been needling me for the past two days.

The truth was, I'd come to care for her, if not love her, and I didn't look forward to Apple's outrage. *Miss Grey's* outrage, I corrected myself.

But her feelings could not matter. Nothing mattered but the sapphire. Hell, I was glad our kiss had been interrupted! I didn't need my attention divided between a smitten-and-rejected, angry as hell damsel in distress and my grand finale.

As we pulled up in the circular drive in front of the grand, gray façade of Maddermark Park, a footman liveried in gold and green approached to take the reins of our team. A second man let down the steps, and a third opened our door. Our own servants had nothing to do but wait for the other two coaches ahead of ours to move out of the way.

Evidently, the other two groups had just arrived, for they were standing in a small knot, chatting on the wide bottom step before the imposing front door.

Before I disembarked, I turned to Miss Grey and her uncle and said, "As fond as I have grown of you both these past days, I must now remember that you are both my servants—and so must you."

Miss Grey stiffened. "Of course," she said in a crisp tone.

Mr. Bird nodded. "You have my loyalty, sir. Nothing but your best interests at heart."

"Thank you." I glanced up at the house. "My first requirement of you is the most important thing I will ask you to do while we are here."

"Which is?" she asked.

I climbed from the coach, praying I hadn't misjudged either of them. "Simply this," I said. "Do not appear surprised at anything that happens in the next ten minutes. If you have questions, remain absolutely impassive and wait to ask them in private."

Miss Grey tilted her head and her eyebrows lowered a couple of suspicious notches, but she emerged from the coach behind me without saying another word.

Immediately, an Instep footman stepped forward and proffered an empty silver salver upon which our footman placed my calling card. Miss Grey's eyes were busy scanning the other two groups of fellow guests, so she didn't understand at first when the Instep footman walked sedately to the front door, glanced at my card, and announced in a loud voice, "Fitzroy Noland, the Viscount Turnbull!"

I saw her eyes widen at mention of the word "viscount," but there was no alarm in her expression, no undue curiosity, and I concluded she either hadn't heard the full name clearly or did not realize she had heard the name Fitzroy Noland before. She peeked around me at the other group, evidently trying to catch a discreet glimpse of the illustrious viscount, which was difficult to do discreetly, since the other guests were now all surreptitiously staring in *our* direction, and for the same reason.

It would have been amusing except that it was not.

"He's a viscount?" Kristen asked. "That jerk! He's toying with her!"

Allison shrugged. "I think it's romantic."

"I think you both need to be quiet," Bernice said a little testily, but everyone excused her, because she was nibbling the last piece of her thirtieth-birthday chocolate. "Go on, Erma."

"Why are they all staring at us?" I murmured and looked up at Mr. Jones, but his eyes were fixed upon an old woman dressed in magenta silk and orange feathers who separated herself from the opposing crowd and approached with frank curiosity and a friendly smile. I decided I liked her at first sight.

She tapped Mr. Jones with her fan. "Turnbull!" she declared. "How grand to meet you at last! I am Ophelia Palin, of Palin House, Grosvenor Square."

Turnbull? Oh, La! As in the Viscount Turnbull? My knees went weak. Mr. Jones wasn't Mr. Jones, but a blinking viscount? I turned to him, my mouth open, but as our eyes met, he pressed his lips together and gave a little shake of his head.

"Of course," I murmured.

He touched my shoulder. "My dear Miss Palin," he addressed the flamboyant old woman, "It gives me great pleasure to introduce you to my fiancée." He turned to me, his face beaming.

"Welcome to England, my dear," Miss Palin said.

I do not remember what happened next. I am told I swooned and that Mr. Jones caught me and carried me into the house. The next thing I knew, I was lying upon a blue damask sofa, my head cradled upon his lap, his fingers stroking my hair, his blue eyes full of concern.

Someone cackled, and I realized I'd drawn a crowd, which discreetly dispersed now that I was conscious—all but Miss Palin, who stopped cackling and cheerfully declared, "What did I tell you, Turnbull? Nothing to fret over." She addressed me next, orange feathers bobbing in her bejeweled turban. "You shall be right enough in a moment, my dear. Do not attempt to stand too quickly. My heavens, but you are both full of surprises! I did not expect to see you here. No one did! Not for another month."

"I was able to book earlier passage from the West Indies to Charleston than I had at first thought I could," he said.

"Of course, of course," she gave a knowing smile. "Couldn't wait to see your lovely wife."

I did sit up too quickly then, swinging my legs to the floor and nearly falling over again. "*Wife?*"

Mr. Jones placed a steadying hand over mine, and his words echoed in my mind. *Do not appear surprised.* I swallowed and shut my mouth.

Miss Palin cackled again and touched my wrist. "Sounds strange, does it? It took my good friend Sally Darlington two years to become used to being referred to as her dear Mr. Darlington's wife. Heavens above, it must seem even more unreal to you, since you married your husband by proxy." She tsked. "Not to fret, though. I suppose you did not realize Turnbull introduced you as his fiancée a moment ago." She shook her head and smiled. "I daresay you both shall slip into your new yoke gently enough. You seem a happy couple. You'll be breeding in no time, my dear, if you are not already—swoons are one sign!—and children are the glue that binds a couple together. Mark my words!" With that, she smiled and floated away, a fluffy magenta cloud, tossing over her shoulder, "Your wife is charming, Lord Turnbull!" She sailed through the door leaving the two of us alone and staring at each other.

"Your *what* is charming, Lord Whoever-You-Blasted-Are!" I hissed. "*Your what?* For I am certain she could not have said, 'wife!'"

He held up his palms. "Believe me, I thought we were only betrothed. I swear I did not know we were married."

"We're *not* married!" I hissed, and then I froze with hideous realization. "You-you are not this Viscount Turnbull, are you? You are playing the imposter! And you brought me here to play the part of the viscount's fiancée!" I put my hands upon my pounding head. "I cannot believe this is happening!" My stomach heaved, and I covered my mouth. "I think I am going to be ill!"

Just then, a footman entered the room, took one look at me and careened about the room searching for something for me to be sick in, finally settling upon a small, pitifully inadequate silver vase, which he handed to me, apologizing the while.

"No, no!" I cried. "It was just a figure of speech! I am not—"

"She is not well," Mr. Jones interrupted. "Pray show us to our bedchamber right away."

My eyes would have shot him a few sharp daggers were they not busy bugging out. I followed woodenly as we were shown upstairs to a chamber. *Our* bedchamber. Our. Bed. Chamber. The one that held the bed that we were supposed to share because we were a married pair! I ransacked my mind for a way out, finding nothing but a plan involving a stolen horse and a large quantity of gin.

"I cannot go in there!" I blurted when we arrived at our

door, which opened like the gaping maw of some giant beast.

"Is there something wrong with the chamber, ma'am?" the footman asked. "I will be happy to—"

"There is nothing wrong with the chamber," said my pretend husband. "Would you please fetch us some refreshment?" He glanced at me. "Milk and some dry toast would be best, I think."

"Of course, my lord."

"I am ill," I stammered. "It-it may be catching. We should sleep in separate chambers."

"'Tis nothing that will not go away on its own in time, my dear," he said, placing his hand against the small of my back and compelling me through the doorway. And then, as the miserably helpful footman launched himself down the hall, my dratted *husband* reached for the door and said, "Eight months should suffice, I think."

Click.

The door shut, and my mouth fell open. "Oh, la! I am with child!"

He turned with a wide smile. "Yes!" he cried. "I admit I did not know what you were about at first, but I caught on soon enough, thank goodness! Couldn't have planned it better myself!"

In two strides, he had me in his arms before I could disabuse him of the notion that a pregnancy was my idea. "Clever Apple!" he cried, picking me up and whirling me about. "I bow to your superior mind! Love it, love it, love it! Absolutely perfect. You are brilliant!" Throwing his head back, he laughed and whirled me around.

The irate set-down I'd been crafting seconds before evaporated like a fog at midday. The only thing I could think of was the press of our bodies. That keen awareness sent all other conscious thoughts scattering until he set me down. And then, framing my face with his hands, he gifted me with a fond smile. "Thank you, Leah!"

The sudden contact broken, I nearly toppled into him.

"Dizzy?" he asked, steadying me with a firm grip.

I nodded though I wasn't dizzy at all. No, he was made of iron, while I'd turned into a blessed magnet. Madness! I pushed away from him and clung to the bedpost instead, the word "love" echoing through my head.

In his voice.

"Cold?" he asked, and I nodded. He pulled the dark green counterpane from the bed and wrapped it about my shoulders. "I sent the footman away in such haste he had no time to tend the fire," he said with a chuckle. "Fortunately, this viscount has had an unconventional education and knows how to tend his own fire."

Still clinging to the post, I sagged to the bed as he removed his coat and bent to the task. He added an oak log to the fire and poked it, and he might have been making a hash of it, for all I knew. I couldn't tear my eyes away from his manly musculature long enough to look!

I'd seen plenty of men. I was an innkeeper, after all, and not some delicate *tonnish* flower. And seeing them with their coats off was nothing new. Heavens, I'd even stumbled upon a few of them naked. But I hadn't been pressed intimately against any of *them*. None of *them* had ever taken me in his arms, twirled me about, or praised my intellect! None of them had been but a breath away from kissing me that morning. And none of them were supposed to be my husband or the father of my child.

What if it were all true?

As I watched, he knelt to poke the fire from a lower angle, his shirt binding across shoulders I hadn't known were that wide or that muscular. Lud, the man was muscular all over. How had I missed that?

Turning a little too suddenly, he caught my eyes enjoying a holiday roaming the hills below his waist. Feigning I'd been woolgathering, my eyes unseeing, I let my lids drift closed and pretended to sway a little.

"Sleepy?" he asked.

"Mmm," I grunted.

"Me too," he said, untying his cravat. "After the foot-man returns with our tray, we'll have a nap." Throwing the folded square of white linen upon the bed, he disappeared into the dressing room, where our trunks had already been deposited. "Unless," he offered, poking his head back into the chamber, "you would care to . . . do something else?" One mischievous eyebrow rose into his cloud of dark curls.

Something else?

Suddenly I realized I was sitting on the bed! An enormous bed! A bed large enough for two. I jumped up, and he laughed.

"What is the matter?" he asked. "Bed not comfortable?" He strode into the room unfastening his cuffs, his shirt half unbuttoned.

"You are not undressing!"

"No," he said, pulling his shirt over his head and revealing an impossibly vast expanse of smooth skin dusted with dark, shiny curls, "and you are not staring."

"I am not staring!" I said, staring. He moved toward the bed and I blinked. "What are you doing now?" I demanded.

"Making good use of my time. I imagine the servants are quite busy just now, what with all the guests arriving at once. Who knows how long our tray will be?" Pulling down the covers, he slid between the sheets. "Mmm . . ." he breathed. "Smooth cotton. This feels good." He patted the other side of the bed and winked, the same gesture I'd seen a thousand times before. "Join me," he said.

"You are mad."

"It is all right. We are married," he said with a mischievous grin.

"We are not!"

"Yes, but they think we are . . . and I locked the door. . . ." Propping his head up on one hand, he smiled indolently. His skin looked impossibly brown against those impossibly white sheets. Suddenly I realized he was covered to the waist and that if I didn't keep my imagination firmly in check, I would find myself imagining he wore nothing beneath those cotton sheets . . . nothing at all . . . skin sliding against crisp, smooth cotton . . .

I realized with a start I was staring again—and that he was wearing a knowing grin.

I pinched the bridge of my nose and groaned, turning away. "Answers!" I blurted. "I want answers. Who are you really, and why are you here? Why am *I* here?"

He sighed. "How very tiresome you are, Apple."

"You did not think so a few minutes ago. I was brilliant, remember? Answer my questions."

"You will not like the answers I give."

I turned back around. "Why am I not surprised?"

He laughed and folded his hands behind his head. "The truth is," he drawled, "that I cannot tell you."

"Rubbish! If one is asked to impersonate a viscountess, one should at least be told the—"

"Ah, but you are not being asked; you are being ordered. Or had you forgotten I am your employer?"

"Not anymore! My chances are better being tried as a pickpocket than as a-a-whatever you have made me now!" The door was only a few steps away, but I never made it. In one fluid motion, he rolled off of the bed and barred my passage.

"Out of my way!" As I tried to push past him, he grasped my waist and pulled me close, close enough to feel the heat radiating from his body, close enough to see the steady beat of his heart pulsing just above his exposed collar bone.

"Please, Apple," he murmured. "Please trust me. I would not ask you to do something harmful or unethical. Please do this. For me."

I hesitated, wanting to believe him, wanting to believe *in* him.

Growing up in The Dancing Maiden had taught me to be a good judge of character. My heart could feel a blackguard even before my head had any concrete proof, and he had never given me a moment's true distress. Each time logic had discovered some apparent flaw in his character, my heart had protested that there had to be some logical explanation, and until now there had been.

But perhaps my head was afraid of my heart's desires. Perhaps it had been looking for something to impugn his character. Perhaps it was time to trust him, as my heart told me I should.

"Did the real viscount put you up to this?" I asked. "Are you playing some sort of madcap hum upon someone? Are you being paid?"

It was his turn to hesitate. After a few seconds of deep breathing and a clenched jaw, he shook his head. I could see little flecks of gold in his eyes, and his voice caressed me as he whispered, "I would tell you if I could, but I cannot. I have given someone my word. And that, my dear Apple, is the truth."

His word. The truth. A scoundrel wouldn't mention either. A scoundrel would make up some fiction to satisfy me. Still, my heart threatened to beat its way out of my chest. "What would happen if we were discovered?"

"We won't be. The real viscount grew up in the West Indies and his bride in Boston," he said. "Neither has ever set foot upon English soil. I have seen the guest list and am certain there are none here who will realize we are imposters."

"How have you seen the guest list? We have only just arrived!"

He cocked his head at a rakish slant and grinned. "I . . . ah . . . had a look at the invitations."

"How?"

He laughed. "It is a long way to London."

"You intercepted the mail!"

"Do not fret; most made it to their destination."

"Most!"

"One or two may have . . . blown away. They were probably for people connected to the viscount."

"Probably?" I scoffed.

He winked and shrugged. "No one here will discover our ruse."

"Unless the real viscount and viscountess show up!"

"She is in Boston as we speak, awaiting the arrival of the viscount, who should be aboard a packet ship bound for Charleston about now. They're not expected in England for at least another month, as Miss Palin said. And by that time the house party will be long over, and Leah Grey will have slipped back into her plain, reassuring life none the worse for the adventure."

I winced and looked down at my hands. "Plain Leah Grey grew up in a country inn, not some rich man's nursery. I cannot possibly pass myself off as a lady!"

"I did not say *you* were plain, Apple, and you will have limited contact with the other guests. Viscountesses spend their time sleeping late, drinking chocolate, eating, and changing clothes five times a day. No one here knows anything about Lady Turnbull. For all they know, she is quite shy, looks exactly like you, and spends her time with her companion at solitary pursuits like walking, riding, or playing chess."

"Companion?" I asked dryly. "I suppose you refer to Miss Cherry."

He grinned. "That's my clever Apple. With Constance to guide you, what can go wrong?"

"Oh, nothing . . . nothing!" I said with a sarcastic lift of my shoulders. "After all, I have served the Quality and know their ways."

"That's the spirit!"

"Right. So, as long as my contact with the other guests is limited to serving them ale, all will be well!"

He smiled. "You underestimate your own abilities. You are lovely, intelligent, and well-spoken. You will have a carefree holiday, and I will have my . . . my little hum, as you call it."

"Well . . . it is not as though we will be stealing their silver," I said. "I imagine there can be no real harm."

"Imagine being waited upon, hand and foot," he said, "night and day, your every whim indulged. Lying abed until noon drinking chocolate . . . seedcakes and pineapple for breakfast . . . having your hair brushed half the day . . ."

I pressed my lips together and closed my eyes. "Mmmm . . . no cooking, no dishes . . ." I couldn't help a dreamy sigh. "It *does* sound nice!"

"So you will help me?"

My eyes refocused. His expression was excruciatingly hopeful, his blue eyes plaintive, his lips slightly open.

I didn't hesitate. "Yes. Yes, I will help you."

"Good girl!" He dropped his hands and exhaled, knowing he'd won.

I took a step back. "But . . . it is too simple. Nothing is that easy."

He threw back his head and laughed. "Oh, my clever Apple! I do like you." He sat on a gold-and-cream striped chair. "You are right, of course. The other guests will be curious about you. You shall have to interact with them at least a little, but you will have Constance to help you, and I daresay she will be able to deflect the most persistent prying."

I sighed and ran my fingertips over a pair of crystal perfume flagons and a small, elaborately worked silver vase sitting on the dressing table and told myself I wouldn't worry. Posthumous Jones was a good man who protected women. He would not put Miss Cherry or me in danger; therefore, whatever his reason for being here, it could not be nefarious.

I concluded the most likely explanation was the viscount himself. There must be someone at the house party the real viscount needed to watch, some intelligence to gather, and he had charged Mr. Jones with the task. Yes, the most logical explanation was that Mr. Jones was there to keep watch.

Of course, curiosity demanded that *I* watch *him*. It would be an amusing diversion to see if I could ferret out his real purpose. I would pay attention to whomever *he* paid attention.

"What is that little smile for, Apple? What mischief are you thinking?"

"Hm? Oh! I . . . was just wondering how late I am able to sleep and if they serve breakfast past noon." I turned away, feeling a little guilty for the lie of omission I'd just told.

"You are frowning now," he observed. "We must play at cards, you and I."

I rolled my eyes and tossed a pillow at him. "I was only wondering . . . where shall we sleep?"

A lazy grin spread over his face, and then, as he rose from the chair, it disappeared, only to be replaced by a feral, predatory expression. Reflexively, I took a step back.

Relentlessly, he advanced, and like a doe about to bolt, I kept stepping back, until I felt the bed bump the backs of my knees. And then my pretend husband leaned forward, enfolding me in an exquisite embrace, lowering me to the soft feather mattress.

"Where shall we sleep?" he murmured. "Why, together, my dear, where all married couples sleep."

CHAPTER TEN

A maid that laughs is half taken.
                    —John Ray, English Proverbs

Her eyes grew to the size of carriage wheels as I lay against her, and I was hard-pressed not to laugh.

"You are jesting, sir!"

I shook my head. "Not at all. I believe I owe you a ravishment." I focused deliberately on her lips and parted my own, but I didn't advance. Instead, I let the seconds slip by. I fully intended to kiss her, but not yet.

She flushed a delightful apple-red and scoffed. "You *are* jesting."

I continued to regard her with a deliberately speculative, deliberately provocative expression. Her eyes opened even wider, and I *did* laugh then. "I have always wondered just how far below your neckline that lovely blush of yours extends. Perhaps I will have a chance to find out."

"I thought you were a gentleman!"

"Make up your mind, Apple. A week ago you knew I was a rake, an hour ago, a paragon. Which is it?" A soft knock sounded on the door.

"Interrupted again," I said, "That will be our tray." I

rolled away from her, and she jumped up like the bed had burnt her backside.

Unlocking the door, I admitted a different footman who gently presented the tray of warm milk and toast to Miss Grey as though she were royalty and made of glass. Clearly word of my wife's interesting condition had spread belowstairs. The footman stammered that the milk had been warmed, announced that supper would be served at nine, "for those who felt up to eating," and beat a hasty retreat, his ears glowing crimson.

I locked the door behind him and smiled.

She scowled. "Am I to eat naught but bread and milk for a fortnight?"

I walked into the dressing room. "Oh, I am sure some weak broth with weak tea could be sent up, if you would like a little variety."

She gasped. "Beast." I heard her laugh at my joke and froze at the sound. I'd not heard her laugh all day—and I realized I'd missed it, by Jove.

"We have three hours until supper," I said. "What say you we nap until then. I am tired."

"Me too," she said.

I heard a suspicious flurry of ruffled sheets and, peeking out of the dressing room, saw that she had lain down—right in the middle of the bed, taking possession of the entire thing. She wasn't going to get away with it.

A few moments later, I emerged from the dressing room deliberately nonchalant in naught but my small clothes, little more than a light breechcloth.

As I'd planned, she screeched and abandoned the middle of the huge bed as I slipped between the sheets—though she didn't leave the bed entirely.

Reaching below the sheets, I pulled my smallclothes away and let them dangle from my fingers. "I sleep in the nude."

Somehow, she dragged her eyes from my smallclothes long enough to toss me a scowl. "I see what you are about," she said, "but you will not win. I am not giving up my side of this bed."

"I will hardly notice. The bed is enormous. I'll wager that two hundred years ago eight people slept on it at a time. A person could get lost on this bed. In the dark, we could be looking for each other and miss."

"Especially if you were sleeping on the floor as any gentleman would offer to do in this situation."

"Well then, thank *goodness* I am no gentleman!"

She frowned, and I actually felt a stab of guilt, which irritated me! "Honestly, Apple, what good would my sleeping on the floor do? It isn't as though your reputation is at stake. No one here knows you. None of the Earl's tonnish guests would ever stop at a place like The Dancing Maiden by choice—assuming they could find it in the first place. It isn't on the road to London or Bath or Brighton or anywhere the beau monde consider civilized."

"What about the servants?"

"What about them? Turned out as you are, you look very different than you did back at The Maiden. Not even your Portman Lowell recognized you. I hardly think one of the Maddermark servants will do better." I folded my hands behind my head. "Admit it, Apple. No one here knows you are an unmarried female. They all think you are a properly wedded and bedded viscountess. So what harm can there possibly be in our sharing a bed so long as I stay on my side and you on yours?"

"A lost night's sleep?"

"Apple!" I grinned. "Are you suggesting my presence in your bed would keep you awake?"

"Do not flatter yourself. There would be nothing exciting about sleeping next to you."

"I am quite equipped to change your mind," I said.

"I do not give a fig about your-your equipment!"

I laughed so hard I didn't even notice she'd picked up a pillow. *Thwack!* A pillow hit the bed between us. *Thunk!*

Another. *Thop!* She placed a final brick in the feather wall between us and slapped it for good measure.

"My side"—she poked the mattress next to her—"your side." She jabbed her finger in my direction. And then, snuffing her candle, she lay down with her back to me.

At that moment, I knew I could have her if I wanted her. Seduction was but an arm's reach and a few whispered endearments away. Which is precisely why I turned over and thought of snow and cold brooks crusted over with ice and pretended to fall asleep. It was an eternity before I actually slept . . .

. . . not a wink, though the bounder taking up all but two inches of my bed went to sleep immediately. I lay awake listening to his breathing even out. I could smell him, a cross between leather and warm caramel. How dare he? Devil take it, men weren't supposed to smell good! La!

Forcing my eyes shut, I told myself I would go to sleep—now! But as I lay there I could feel a heart beating, and I realized I wasn't sure whose it was! Suddenly the reassuringly substantial wall of pillows between us seemed to dissipate into the moon-shadows, and I found myself sleeping in bed with an alarmingly naked man. An alarmingly attractive naked man.

I tried not to think of what he didn't have on under the counterpane. Instead, I imagined him wearing a full suit of armor—a fancy that worked well until he turned over and I heard the bed linen glide over his skin. As a last resort, I counted sheep and was nearly asleep when I realized the dratted things were jumping directly over his fabled equipment—and one of them tripped on it.

CHAPTER ELEVEN

*Not all those who know their minds know their hearts as
well.*

> —François, Duc De La Rochefoucauld

I awoke on the floor. Breathing hurt, rolling over hurt,
and a sudden light stabbed my eyes as some bedlamite
opened the draperies and trilled a disgustingly cheerful,
"Good morning!"

I opened my eyes a crack. "Miss Cherry?"

"I am Constance to my friends, *chérie*, and as we are to
be bosom companions for the fortnight, I think it wise that
you use it. Besides, I have taken quite a great liking to you.
You are . . . worthy."

Wiping the tell-tale moisture from my cheek, I certainly
did not feel worthy! Miss Cherry—*Constance!*—wore a
blindingly white walking dress trimmed in green satin and
a wide smile. I sat up feeling rumpled and out-of-sorts and
looked to the bed, which still bore the impression of Mr.
Jones's large body. The bounder had reigned over the
kingdom of the bed all night, while I had crept soundlessly
to the floor, feeling like the coward I was.

Miss Cherry cooed comfortingly. "Long night?"

"What time is it?" I mumbled, my mouth full of cotton.

"Almost noon." Walking to the bed, she busied herself with a tea tray that waited there. "This is still warm, I think, though it is a little weak, and the toast is dry. We shall have to put it about that you are over the morning sickness or you shall starve!" She laughed.

I groaned and covered my face with my hands. "Do the servants all know about . . . about my interesting condition?"

"Oh, yes! Everyone does. Apparently, the word passed among the guests in whispers over breakfast."

"Oh, la! Have you seen Mr. Jones?"

"Pos? Indeed. He retrieved me from the maid's quarters in the garret early this morning."

"The garret!"

She laughed when I cringed. "The place was not as cold, drafty, and overpopulated as the servants would have you believe. It was actually quite comfortable, though I am to have the adjoining room tonight."

"The adjoining room? Do companions and ladies' maids not usually sleep on a cot in the dressing room?"

"Indeed, but the viscount would not hear of it. He insisted that I have the adjoining bedchamber; the viscount can be quite a persuasive man."

"What viscount?"

"Why, yours, *chérie!*"

"Oh. Yes. I forgot."

She laughed. "Your head is still stuffed with cotton. You must not have slept much—not that any lady could with Posthumous Jones in her bed."

My head cleared instantly, and I scrambled to my feet, my back complaining. "We did not sleep in the same bed!"

"Of course not." She gave a raised-eyebrow smile. "I cannot imagine either of you *slept.*"

"Miss Cherry!"

"Come now," she said, handing me a cup of tea, "we are both women, and you cannot look me in the eye and say you do not find him attractive." She gave me a penetrating look. "You do, do you not?"

I gave a reluctant, exasperated, and awkward nod of my head. "Well . . . yes! I do . . . a little. But that does not mean that-that I would-that we—"

"Played a little game of seek-and-find?"

My tea—how shall I put it?—sprayed oh-so-delicately from my nose. "No!" I cried.

"Oh!" Constance said. "I am sorry. I was under the impression that that is what you both wanted."

"No!"

"My mistake then." She lowered her eyes and took a demure sip of her own tea.

I hurried into the dressing room, her words swirling around in my head like confused bees. After washing hastily and pulling my hair into a knot at the nape of my neck, I dressed in a light blue calico walking dress and soft, low boots. "Ah . . . Miss Cherry . . ."

"Constance?"

"Oh, yes. Constance . . ."

"Yes, *chérie?*"

"Do you really think that Pos—that Mr. Jones has formed some sort of attachment?"

"But of course!"

Emerging from the dressing room, I examined her lovely face. Somehow the lines etched there only made her look more mysterious, more charismatic. She had the sort of eyes that saw everything, the sort of mind that could make sense of it all, and the sort of heart that made it feel safe to confide in her. "What makes you so certain?"

"I have known him a long time."

"Since he was a boy."

Her eyes widened. "Is that what he told you?"

"No." I shook my head and picked up my teacup. "On the way here I saw the medallion he toys with up close. I'd learned what they signify from our mermaid, Miss Sarah Brown, and that coupled with all that false name claptrap and his brotherly relationship to the ladies of The Birdhouse made it easy to hazard a guess about his origins."

She nodded and poured herself some more tea. "No wonder he loves you. You are clever and kind, a . . ."

I have no idea what she said next, for I stared into my teacup, hearing not a word of it. Love? Could that be right? Did Pos love me?

Pos! In my mind, I addressed him that way, starting right then. No more Mr. Jones. No more Posthumous Jones. Just Pos, Pos who loved me—if Constance was right.

"—and you do not want that, do you?"

I startled. "Oh, Constance, I am sorry. I was not attending."

"Forgiven, *chérie*. It is not everyday a young lady realizes she is in love with a handsome young man."

"Oh, but we are not . . . I mean, it is not what you think."

She threw me a speaking glance and said, "I think nothing, *chérie,* but you, you perhaps should do some thinking of your own."

"What do you mean?"

"Only that I wish you to remember that even the strongest heart can be broken."

"My heart is in no danger," I said at last.

"I was not speaking of yours," she said, pulling on her gloves. "Come. It is a glorious day. Let us escape into the warm sunshine and the cool air!" Sweeping up an elegant, wide brimmed bonnet from the bed, she sailed through the door and down the hall, leaving me with nothing to do but retrieve my own gloves and bonnet and follow her. How else was I going to find Pos?

We hadn't even reached the stairs when my hopes were dashed. A footman told us the gentlemen had all ventured forth for a day of sport, which meant shooting, I presumed. I was disappointed and pretended not to notice the sympathetic look Constance cast at me.

Making for the terrace, we had just stepped through the tall glass doors when we heard a pair of twin giggles above our heads that gave pause to our footsteps. We looked up in surprise, the sound flying onto the breeze from a window one level above. Constance and I traded smiles.

"What do you suppose 'e'll dress like tomorrow, Mary?" asked one, letting her accent show through her carefully crafted service English. She obviously thought the moment private, and Constance and I headed silently down the wide, curving terrace stairs, but we couldn't help hearing the rest of the conversation, regardless.

"I don't know," Mary said, laughing. "His Majesty, maybe—or perhaps a pirate!"

The other woman squealed. "Go, on! A pirate!"

"Why not? He's already ransacked the attic, and who knows what other sort of costumes are up there? And he looks daft enough for it to me. That get-up 'e's got on today is worse than that, ain't it?"

"I wonder how 'e gets away with it."

"I'll wager he wasn't that way when he was hired. Probably been with the viscount since God wore nappies." At mention of the word viscount, we stopped again, unable to help listening, and the maid went on talking. "Sometimes the Quality really are quality," she said, "and that viscount is a right 'un. Do you know 'e marched into the kitchen this morning and poured himself a cup—right with 'is own two 'ands!"

"I was there. Surprised the bubble and squeak out o' me," Mary agreed. "Too bad he's married!" She giggled.

"Oh, la!" her counterpart cried in an exaggeratedly proper voice. "It is a pity, is it not? For we penniless, common chambermaids are in *such* short supply, and charming, handsome-as-sin viscounts need sturdy women to help them carry their burdens!"

"Burdens like charm, money, and looks?"

"Exactly!"

They both laughed gaily and moved away from the window, apparently, for their voices faded. It was all Constance and I could do to keep from laughing ourselves. We hurried down the stairs and out onto the lawn. "La,

Zebra Contemporary

If the FREE Book Certificate is missing, call 1-800-770-1963 to place your order.
Be sure to visit our website at www.kensingtonbooks.com.

FREE BOOK CERTIFICATE

Yes!

Please send me FREE Zebra Contemporary romance novels. I only pay $1.99 for shipping and handling. I understand that each month thereafter I will be able to preview 4 brand-new Contemporary Romances FREE for 10 days. Then, if I should decide to keep them, I will pay the money-saving preferred subscriber's price (that's a savings of up to 30% off the retail price), plus shipping and handling. I understand I am under no obligation to purchase any books, as explained on this card.

Name _____

Address _____ Apt. _____

City _____ State _____ Zip _____

Telephone ( ) _____

Signature _____
(If under 18, parent or guardian must sign)

Thank You!

CN095A

THE BENEFITS
OF BOOK CLUB
MEMBERSHIP

- You'll get your books
  hot off the press,
  usually before they
  appear in bookstores.

- You'll ALWAYS save
  up to 30% off the
  cover price.

- You'll get our FREE
  monthly newsletter
  filled with author
  interviews, book
  previews, special
  offers and MORE!

- There's no obligation
  — you can cancel at
  any time and you have
  no minimum number
  of books to buy.

- And—if you decide
  you don't like the
  books you receive,
  you can return them.
  (You always have ten
  days to decide.)

IIl..l.lll....ll.l.l.l.l..l.l.ll.l.l...lll.ll...l

Zebra Contemporary Romance Book Club
Zebra Home Subscription Service, Inc.
P.O. Box 5214
Clifton , NJ 07015-5214

PLACE
STAMP
HERE

but that was funny!" I cried when we were safely out of earshot. "But I wonder who they were talking about?"

"I do not know. I wonder if my driver and footman are putting on airs. I fancy they were a bit jealous over the Instep livery. Perhaps they've put together some sort of livery of their own?"

I shrugged. "Should we speak with them about it?"

She shook her head. "Let them be. I am sure it cannot matter."

We walked on in silence for a time, enjoying the fresh breeze and the sunshine. Everything seemed nicer here, the grass greener, the clouds fluffier. The very air was perfumed with the scent of summer, and everything seemed cleaner, somehow. We wandered among a neatly kept parterre and had just passed through a vast boxwood labyrinth when Constance cried, "Heavens! Look at that!"

There in the distance was a woman, a shepherdess. "She's dressed like Bo Peep!"

"At least she's dressed the part," Constance said. "She certainly does not act it!"

The poor thing had her sheep going every which way, and she was flailing her hook around and running after the beasts.

"Let us go help her." Constance said.

"Do *you* know anything about herding sheep?"

"No, but it looks fun!" she said with a chuckle. "Besides, how else are we to find out who that woman really is? For she is certainly *not* a real shepherdess!"

"Lead on!"

Muttering and shouting the while, the shepherdess was too busy to notice our approach. The sheep weren't cooperating. As we neared, she threw down her hook and cried in a very odd, low voice, "Damn you mutton! I will eat you for dinner!"

Constance and I gasped, and the shepherdess wheeled around to stare at us, her wig falling off.

"Uncle!" I was tempted to pinch myself. "What in God's name are you doing?"

"Shh!" He looked around as though there might be spies hiding behind the trees. "Call me . . . ah . . . Gwendolyn!" he whispered.

"Why are you dressed as a shepherdess, *mon cher?*" Constance asked.

"We are all incognito!" Uncle said, as though that explained everything. "We must remain inconspicuous! Please, go about your walk! Shoo! Shoo!"

We weren't sure if he were speaking that last to the sheep or to us. He picked up his hook and moved off.

"Come," Constance said. "That copse of birch trees looks pleasant enough. Let us do as Mr. Bird says."

"We cannot just leave him here like that!"

"Why not?" Constance asked. "He is a grown man. I fancy he can take care of himself."

I followed her, shaking my head, into the copse, where a footpath dappled by sunlight meandered among the trees. At first glance, the copse was apparently wild, yet obviously groomed to look that way. Tight patches of wildflowers and stone benches were scattered here and there along an easy path that wound down a gentle hillside. Coming into a wide clearing, my breath caught at the sight of a pond with a pair of perfect white swans floating on its glassy blue surface and a white marble temple reflecting off the water from the far side. We might have been in ancient Greece or on Mount Olympus. I couldn't help thinking what it must have been like to grow up in such a place. The parterre, the labyrinth, the wood—all wonderful places for children to play. And the meadow with its pond and temple were at once remote, but with the stone battlements at the corners of the oldest part of the earl's house peeking reassuringly over the tops of the trees.

"La, can you imagine living in such grandeur every day?" I murmured.

"Yes, *chérie,* I can," Constance said quietly.

I closed my eyes, realizing my error. Of course she could imagine it. She had lived it. "Forgive me. I had forgotten everything was taken away from you."

"Not everything." She bent to pick a bluebell. "Real flowers are prettier than flowers made of silver."

"True."

"The happiest people are those who understand that beauty does not hinge on an object's monetary value."

"Or a person's monetary value."

She gave a soft smile and nodded. "Smart girl." She sighed. "I am happier than I have ever been in my life, my dear. Your uncle—"

"My lady!" an Instep footman called from the copse behind us, and for a moment I wondered who he meant.

"Lady Turnbull," Constance said, "I believe the footman requires your attention."

"Oh!" I turned to the man. "Yes. Ah . . . yes?"

"Begging your pardon, my lady, but your husband has returned from the hunt, and he has been injured!"

Erma closed the books and yawned. "It's late."

A chorus of dismay spearheaded a swift protest. "You can't leave us hanging like that!" Tamara grumbled.

"I cannot go on reading," Erma said. "My voice is cracking."

"I'll read!" Stephanie volunteered. "Is that okay?"

"Oh, yes! Stephanie reads great," Kristen said.

"Well," Erma corrected. "Stephanie reads well."

"Yes. She reads well. Splendidly. Incomparably. Masterfully. Exquisitel—"

"All right!" Erma said, holding up one hand and laughing. "I get the point. Stephanie may continue the tale in my stead. But if I fall asleep, don't wake me with your sobbing."

"Sobbing?" Tamara cried.

Amy scoffed. "She's only teasing, the dragon. Aren't you, Erma?"

"Only one way to find out," the old woman said. "Read on, Stephanie!"

When I arrived back at Maddermark Park, I was rushed to our bedchamber, where I saw a still form in the bed with a man and a gray haired woman hovering nearby.

"What happened?" I exclaimed, rushing to the bed.

The man took me by the shoulders and whispered, "A fall down a rocky embankment, Lady Turnbull. He suffered a blow to the head."

Tears pricked my eyes. "Is he . . . ?"

"Dead? Oh, no, no! Merely dosed with laudanum."

"Thank God!" My knees gave way, and the next thing I knew, I was sitting in a heap on the floor beside the bed, sobbing. "Oh, dearest! Please . . . you mustn't leave me."

"Now, now . . ." the doctor cooed, patting my shoulder. "He will be right soon enough, I expect. As luck would have it, I was a member of the hunting party—I am Doctor Adams—and I was able to treat him straightaway. Now then—come away, Lady Turnbull. Such disturbances are not good for the child."

I followed his gaze down to my belly. "Oh!" I'd forgotten. "Do not be concerned. I am certain I will be fine. I am more worried about-about my husband. Are you sure he will be all right?"

"Of course I cannot say with one hundred–percent assurance. He took a nasty blow to the head—"

"On the back of his head? I don't see a bandage . . ."

"There was no blood or even a contusion," said the doctor. "Nevertheless, I am certain of my diagnosis, for he was raving and when we brought him—"

"Raving!"

"I am afraid so, Lady Turnbull. Quite out of his head, but I cured him with an immediate bleeding and the dose of laudanum. He is resting comfortably, now, Lady Turnbull. It is best you leave him and attempt to rest as well. You are to have the adjoining room."

"Out of the question!"

"—and I have left strict instructions for you to be kept away from him until he is completely recovered. Emotional disturbances are vastly injurious to ladies in your condition. You really must leave. I insist."

"I am staying. *You* are leaving."

"But—"

"*I* insist."

"Best do as she says," the lady said—in a familiar voice!

I spun around and saw that the person I'd assumed was a lady was no lady! It was Uncle, dressed in a long, black robe and a judge's wig! But I had no time to question him on his strange attire.

He waggled his finger at the physician. "If you think she's excited now, you just try to make her leave his side. She loves him, and she'll fight like a wildcat to be with him. Saw her do it before, when we made the crossing from America and pirates set upon our ship!" He whistled.

"Pirates!" the doctor said.

Uncle nodded at me. "Sure enough. And I swear on a stack of holy books it's because o' her we escaped. She seems a quiet, biddable little thing, but it would be a mistake to let that fool you. Once she gets riled, as she is now," he said pointedly, "well, she ain't exactly quiet any more." He laughed in an anxious manner. "Women from Boston, you know. . . ." He let his voice trail off ominously, as though "women from Boston" were synonymous with "hounds of hell."

Uncle met my eyes, and I looked up at the doctor, opened my eyes wide, and growled a little.

He opened his eyes even wider and edged away. "I, ah . . . if you think it best. You know them both better than I." His shaking fingers made contact with the door latch. "I-I will check on him later."

Click. The door closed behind him.

I turned to Uncle. "Pirates?"

"Worked didn't it?" He chuckled and moved to the door. "Heading to the kitchen. I expect our patient will be hungry when he wakes up. I'll bring a meal, something that will keep until the laudanum wears off. I will smuggle something up for you, too. My grand-nephew needs more than toast and milk." With that, he quit the room in a swirl of black baize, his wig flapping, and I was left alone with the unconscious Mr. Jones.

He was covered in a heap of blankets, propped against a heap of feather pillows. I didn't know if it was his condition or the contrast of his dark hair against the white pillowcases, but his skin looked pale. My breath caught in my throat. "Oh, Mr. Jones," I whispered. He didn't move. "Oh, Posthumous . . . Pos!" I dashed a tear from my eye. "You mustn't leave me. I still grieve over my parents. When they were robbed and murdered, I wanted to die, too. I do not think my heart could bear the grief of you being taken from me, too. Not now." I sighed and bowed my head, resting it lightly against his side and closing my eyes, inhaling his scent, listening to the steady rhythm of his breathing.

"You . . . you have captured my heart," I confessed to the sleeping man. "But I think you did it long ago. I think I have loved you since the day you first set foot inside The Dancing Maiden." I looked at his pale face, tears streaming down my cheeks. And then a sudden smile welled up from somewhere deep inside, and I chuckled through my sobs. "I love you, you bounder, and you dare not die now, for you owe me a ravishing, damn it!"

I'd known since the moment we'd met that she was at least a little fascinated with me, but I'd had no idea her feelings had grown beyond the naturally curious. I'd always thought we might entertain each other for an afternoon someday. And an hour ago I would have been

happy to oblige her and grant her the ravishing of a lifetime. But when the word love came whispering from her
lips, it raked across old wounds, opening my raw desires,
old hurts I thought had healed.

Love, the prerequisite to wife, family, home, and happiness. Love, for which I was singularly unworthy. "I love
you," she'd said through laughter and tears, a symphony
of heart and hope and fear matching my own, and for a
moment, I forgot everything else—my plan, the gem, my
mother, my misdeeds, even where we were.

"Dear Apple," I said, reaching to caress her cheek.

She looked up, and a smile blossomed upon her face,
the sheer joy in it lighting my entire existence. "You are
awake!"

"Indeed." I smiled.

"And you are not asleep!" Her eyes went wide, and she
looked horrified. Clearly, she was wondering how much
I'd heard.

"I am recovered," I said. "Completely. It is a miracle."

"But-but the doctor gave you laudanum! You are not
supposed to be awake!"

"Alas I am afraid that is what happens when one does
not swallow one's laudanum. I spit it out."

Her brows slammed together. "Then you were only
pretending to be asleep!"

I shrugged. "Guilty." I grinned, wondering whether
to needle her about owing her a ravishment or to make
a few romantic confessions of my own.

"How dare you?" she demanded, anger having replaced her grief of a moment before. I was delighted! I
laughed out loud. Suddenly, the clouds parted, and I realized I was about to tell her everything. Here, at last, was
the woman with whom I could share my life. She would
understand. She would see the sapphire was rightfully
mine and that robbing the earl of it was not really thievery at all but—

I stilled.

Robbery. Her words of a few moments before swirled and coalesced in my mind. *"When they were robbed and murdered . . . "* Dear God, her parents had been killed by thieves!

My blood ran cold.

No wonder Apple—rational, reasonable Apple—had been so vehement every time I'd suggested her Uncle was a thief. She hated thieves. She would hate me, as soon as she found out I was a thief. And that I meant to make her one, too.

"Well? What have you to say?" she prompted. "Pretending to be drugged! Why would you do such a thing?"

I pasted on a callous grin. "How else to coax from you a sweet declaration of love? Now then"—I rubbed my lap lewdly and winked, clearly insulting her, shocking her, hurting her—"come sit upon my lap. I believe I owe you a ravishing."

She ran like a striped ass, and I didn't try to stop her. Why would I? My words had been calculated to drive her away.

Not caring if anyone saw, I stalked to the door and gave the key a savage turn. I'd spent a lifetime lying—what was one more lie? Turning to the basin, I splashed cold water on my face and took a deep breath, but lying to her still felt wrong. A flask of brandy in my valise provided a welcome burn to focus upon. I unlocked the door and lay down once more, contemplating the bland, white ceiling. I missed the peacocks roosting in the painted tree that graced the ceiling of my chamber back at The Birdhouse. It had been my mother's room. How she would have loved Apple!

Squeezing my eyes shut, I tried not to think about either of them. The sapphire was at last within my grasp. I planned to take it that night, when everyone else was slumbering, and replace it with the fake. It was an excellent copy and would fool everyone for as long as necessary, I was sure, but if it were discovered before we could come away, still none would suspect me. A laudanum-induced stupor was the perfect alibi.

I really had fallen on the hunt, though it wasn't anything serious—just a slip down an embankment, but I'd seen an opportunity and taken it. I'd been planning to head back to the estate early, anyway, begging a megrim or some such claptrap. It wasn't the manly thing to do, but I didn't have to worry after my reputation, since I wasn't the real viscount, and soon everyone would know *he* hadn't really been here at all, so his reputation wasn't in danger, either.

I wondered what it would be like to be the real viscount, to own vast estates I'd never even glimpsed. I'd seen one of the Viscount Turnbull's estates once. What would it be like to come home to such a place, knowing it was mine forever. I wondered if his chest would swell with pride as he presented it to his lady wife as he handed her down from their coach and her dainty slipper touched ground that had been in the possession of his family for centuries.

I shook my head and sighed. In London, my mother and I lived in a series of tiny, dim rooms in others' houses, and after I lost her I lived with a street gang in alleyways or in the dank basements of flash houses, when we were lucky. Before I'd come here, I'd intended to settle after this, to build a tidy little cottage in the country near The Birdhouse and spend the rest of my days helping Constance carry out her mission, which was worthy and right. She and her charges were as close to family as I had, as close as I would ever have, but I wasn't worthy of them or of Leah Grey. I never would be. I was a thief. I'd lived in the shadows, witnessed dark things, done dark things. I could not atone. My life was stained and could never be washed clean. Not clean like her.

She was perfect, like the gem.

My mother's sapphire. How ironic that the most valuable thing I'd ever steal—and the last!—was something rightfully mine to begin with!

John Bird came bumping into the room before long, carrying a laden tray. I closed my eyes and feigned sleep until he withdrew to the dressing room, closing the door behind him. Soon, he was snoring softly.

I closed my eyes then and really did try to go to sleep. I needed to be alert for later. But instead of sleeping, I listened over and over in my mind to Apple's declaration of love. Apple, who feared thieves, hated them, *loathed* them. Apple, who would become an accomplice to thievery the moment I recovered the gem. How could I do that to her?

How could I not?

I was doing her a favor.

CHAPTER TWELVE

Love sought is good, but given unsought, is better.
                    —William Shakespeare

I charged blindly down the hall and reached the top of the stairs before realizing I had nowhere to go. Clutching at a heavily carved baluster, I dashed at a tear with my sleeve. "How dare you make me cry!"

"Why, what is wrong, my dear?" a voice echoed upward from the shadowed landing below. A small woman stood there, shrouded in black and regarding me through a heavy black lace veil. "What dastard has made you cry?" she asked, climbing the stairs. "Shall I call for someone?" Reaching my side, she touched my hand. Even standing next to her, I could barely see her eyes.

"No." I shook my head. "No. It is nothing."

"Nothing! Pish-tosh. Tears are never nothing. You would be well not to forget that—and not to let *him* forget it, either." I must have given her a startled look, for she chuckled. The sound seemed incongruous with her deep mourning attire. In fact, her very presence at a house party was incongruous with deep mourning attire.

She gestured vaguely. "Would you like some tea, perhaps? I am heading for my chamber, but I could meet you in one of the parlors, if you can find me—this place has seven of them! Or so I hear," she added. "Oh, but, perhaps you would not like to appear in public just now . . . and you cannot go back to your own chamber, clearly, so perhaps my chamber would be best, and—*la!*—where are my manners? We have not been introduced. I am Eliza Mapes, Mrs. Eliza Mapes."

Before thinking, I bobbed a curtsy, and she laughed. "My, you *are* new to all this, Lady Turnbull!"

"You know who I am?"

"Is there a soul who does not?" She took me by the arm and led me down the hall. "Now then, I shall take you under my wing, my little American darling, whether you like it or not; for you remind me of my dear daughter. I can tell you've a good heart, just like she had, and I wouldn't have wanted her to be thrown to the wolves as you clearly have been. You need someone to guide you, someone who does not share the silly bigotry of the silly *ton* but who understands it nonetheless. I am afraid even a viscountess would fare poorly among them if she went about curtsying to every Tom, Dick, and footman. Do they not teach such things in Boston? But of course not; you Americans curtsy to everyone for 'all men are created equal' right? Sly Mr. Jefferson. I think he knew very well women are created superior!" She laughed. "Women who want to be equal to men lack imagination!"

I couldn't help smiling a little.

"Really, now, here in England you must not curtsy to anyone below you on the social ladder, my dear, and I am quite below you. My husband was a mere Mr., and—"

She stopped for a breath, and I blurted, "I am sorry for your loss!"

"Oh, no!" she responded. "You misunderstand. I am not a grieving widow, my dear, but a grieving mother. My daughter." She placed her palm over a large locket that hung over her heart. "Taken by a fever last year. Would you like to see her?" Without waiting for a reply, she opened the locket, revealing a portrait of a young blonde girl with striking blue eyes. "We named her Sapphire after those eyes. They were that color the day she was born. Ah, here we are!" Opening a door, she drew me into her bedchamber. "Do sit down in front of the fire, and I will ring for tea."

What else could I do? I sat.

Some women are born mothers. Kindness and warmth surround them, enveloping those in need like a tender embrace. You have only to stand in their presence for seconds to know without doubt their compassion is genuine, that they will accept your faults even as they point them out. They know how you are feeling before you recognize it yourself, and they share your pain or joy as though it were their own. Mrs. Mapes was one of those, and though I'd met many women like her in the years since my mother's death, I hadn't been the object of their motherly attention until the moment Mrs. Mapes locked the door, took off her veil, and looked at me, her head cocked to one side.

I felt uncomfortable under her gaze, as though she could see all of my secrets, but somehow I knew she was the type who would keep them even as she advised me to reveal them, so I tried to relax and let the seconds tick by.

"You seem a good girl," she said at last. "Your mother must be very proud."

I couldn't keep my face from crumpling just a little.

"Oh, you poor darling," she soothed, handing me a handkerchief. "I can see you miss her very much."

I nodded. It was the truth; I did miss my mama. Uncle was a dear and he loved me, but there was no substitute for a mother's loving touch. Looking up, I gave her a tremulous smile. "Very much," I agreed.

"Well," she said, giving the bell rope a pull, "I cannot produce your mama, but there is very little evil in this world a cup of hot tea and a biscuit or two cannot set at some distance, at least for a few minutes. I will send for a tray and we will pretend the world does not exist until you decide what to do next. Now then"—she wet and wrung out a towel at the basin and brought it to me—"put this on your face child. No man is worth puffy eyes. My daughter loved to have her hair brushed when she was upset. Do you?"

I smiled, and she got busy, chattering the while. Her daughter had died almost one year ago, but Mrs. Mapes still wore mourning clothes and always would, she declared, though clearly she had moved on. Cheerful and lively, she was quick to laugh, and before long my spirits lifted. She brushed my hair and then tea arrived, and we spent a good part of the afternoon chatting while she pinned my hair into different configurations atop my head, first elegant and then ridiculous. We spoke of many things, both serious and silly.

Now, I was and am a woman of honor and I'd promised to help Posthumous Jones, which meant keeping his secrets, even if he was an insufferable cad. But life at The Dancing Maiden had taught me to be a good judge of character, and I knew Mrs. Mapes would keep what I said to herself as surely as I knew my own mother would have. Along with hot tea, she served cold disdain for anything and anyone who might cause me harm, and it wasn't long before I was confessing at least a part of my troubles.

After my last disastrous encounter with Mr. Jones, I needed someone in whom to confide. Constance was already Mr. Jones's confidant, and Uncle was . . . well, a *man!* And Mrs. Mapes? She was a miracle!

Still, I did not tell her everything. Nothing about our false identities or why we were here—not that I knew myself, as Pos hadn't shared that with me. But I did share with her my lover's woes. I told her about "his lordship" repeatedly inviting me to sit upon his lap. I told her about the pink gown and how he had acted as though he were unimpressed and unaffected even though my companion—Constance—was sure he was very much affected and just didn't want to admit it. I told her about my "husband" almost kissing me the day before. And finally, I told her of my humiliating confession of love to an unconscious man who was very much conscious!

"I do not know if I was more angry or more hurt," I said some time later between sips of tea. "Clearly, he heard my foolish declaration, and just as clearly he does not return my feelings—though the scapegrace is not above exploiting them for the purpose of ravishment, should I be willing."

"Men often hide their feelings, my dear. Perhaps you should let more time pass before you decide he does not return yours. Your companion seems to think you have some power over him, else she would not have been smiling at his behavior over the pink gown."

"What possible reason could he have for keeping his feelings a secret?"

"Perhaps you should ask him that," she said gently.

"I will. Tonight."

"In bed?"

I looked at her sharply. "I thought you understood. We have not . . . yet . . ."

"I understood. Oh, yes! But . . . my dear . . . I doubt it has escaped you that you are four-and-twenty and still unplucked."

"Still unkissed!"

"Exactly. And you must be as curious as the next healthy young woman about what passes between men and women."

I looked at my hands and shrugged.

She sighed. "That is what I thought. And that's natural enough; every other married lady has gone through what you are going through—just not for so long. Most ladies suffer this kind of suspense only between the wedding and the wedding night. Your husband is derelict in his duty."

I squirmed in my chair a little. The conversation had

taken an alarming turn! "Mm," I murmured, not knowing what to say—or what not to say.

"Perhaps you should try sitting on his lap once or twice."

I gasped and looked up at her, and she shrugged. "Just a thought," she said with a smile, pouring more tea. "What have you to lose but your unassuaged curiosity?"

I changed the subject and she allowed it, and I excused myself soon after, but not before she'd extracted a promise to come to her chamber again the next afternoon. Escaping into the garden, I made for the serenity of the little meadow Constance and I had discovered that morning.

I wanted nothing more than to avoid *him* the rest of the day—which would be easy, I thought, as he was abed in our chamber affecting a laudanum-induced stupor.

Why? I ransacked my brain for a reasonable explanation for such odd behavior. If he were present to act as the real viscount's eyes or ears, why was he holed up in our bedchamber affecting illness? I couldn't understand it, and I was intensely curious, but I couldn't bear more of the bounder's teasing, and I wasn't going anywhere near that bedchamber until I absolutely had to.

And when I arrived, I didn't know if I'd interrogate him or strangle him. Sitting in the drowsy afternoon silence of the clearing's little temple, watching the swans snooze on the grassy shore, I thought back to the way I'd sobbed when I thought he'd died that morning. La, what a ninny I was! I hardly knew anything about him apart from his manly appetite. How many times had he tried to tempt me onto his lap? What did I see in him? Nothing. Nothing at all. I didn't know him. How could I? Mr. Viscount was a liar, that much was clear, and I couldn't be sure of anything he said or did.

It wasn't reasonable to fall in love with him. It wasn't logical. It wasn't practical.

That was that. I would not love him.

I spent the next three hours believing that I could fall out of love as easily as I'd fallen into love. I didn't suppose

he would come to supper that night, but I would explain my decision when I saw him later that night in our
chamber. I would be matter-of-fact. Sensible. Adamant.

I would explain that my words had been shaped by
shock. He'd been a friendly, if troublesome, fixture in my
life for a long time and I'd thought he was dead. I cared
for him, in a very non-passionate way. Sobbing out that
I loved him had been a silly, emotional reaction. Nothing more. I did not love him. Not really.

It didn't matter that his lies had begun as a way to obscure his origins as a lad, that lying had been as essential
to him as breathing, that caution was second nature to him.

Truth was right and lying was wrong. It was a distinct
divide. That's the way it had always been, and that's the
way I liked it. Nothing left open to interpretation. Black
and white, just as he'd said. No shades of gray. There
wasn't a thing wrong with that!

Yes. Everything would still work out well, I was sure. Two
weeks from then, I would be back at The Maiden and
everything would be back to normal.

Orderly. Constant. Routine. Comforting.

On the second night, we had our first formal supper
of the house party. The first night had seen late arrivals,
and it was considered impolite to rush them to make an
appearance before they'd enjoyed a full night of sleep,
and so, while the guests had been strolling the grounds
and talking among themselves, we had not yet been formally welcomed by our host.

The guests gathered in the summer parlor just before
nine-o'-the-clock, but I was a few minutes late and made
my apologies to the assembled company, for the procession into supper had been delayed as I was the second
highest ranking gentleman of the company after the earl
himself.

I'd become lost, I told everyone, which wasn't difficult

130 *Melynda Beth Skinner*

to believe, as Maddermark Park was an enormous place, and its cavernous, twisty halls seemed to stretch forever. Sympathetic murmurs rose from the assembly, and that was the end of it.

Everyone wore their finest clothing, and upon entering the sumptuous parlor resplendent in blue and gold, a sea of colors dazzled my eyes. Silk of every hue had been used to construct the ladies' gowns it seemed. I love bright color, and that night's array was as breathtaking as any I'd ever seen. Yet somehow my gaze was drawn to just one color, to just one lady. Leah. She was standing there in the company of an older lady in mourning, which was strange enough in itself, but the arch smile she wore perplexed me even more—until I realized she was wearing a watered silk the exact color of an apple. Clever girl.

"I take it you have forgiven me," I said, gaining her side.

"Not at all. But I do not see a point in us being anything but amiable, do you?"

"We have always been so, and I trust we always shall be, Apple."

The earl began the formal procession into the grand dining salon with Countess Rangnor, as the highest ranking lady present, on his arm.

I held out my arm to Apple. "Shall we?"

She took my arm and walked sedately beside me, and I couldn't help smiling. She was as level-headed as they came. After the way I'd treated her, I'd expected her to be angry with me, but she wasn't. At least she did not *appear* to be.

As we walked in to the dining hall, I considered the man in front of me. The earl had surprised me. I'd come here predisposed to dislike him, even to hate him. That wasn't rational, of course. It came from the depths of my soul. He had my mother's sapphire! But the Earl of Instep wasn't at all what I'd expected. He smiled often. He was amiable, even garrulous. And he wasn't in the least haughty, as I'd come to expect from members of the *haute ton*.

Not for the first time, I wondered how he had come to be in possession of the "Instep Sapphire." That name galled me. It shouldn't be called that. It had been my mother's sapphire.

And it soon would be mine!

Even with us desperately poor, as I know we had to have been when I was a tiny lad, she'd never sold the stone. Instead, nearly every day, she'd hold it up on its golden chain for me so I could watch it sparkle in the sunlight, and smile.

"Can I have it, Mama?"

"Someday," she'd say. "I hope, someday."

We all took our places around the long dining table and sat, but after the first wine was poured, the earl stood up, holding up his palm for us to remain seated.

"I wish to make an announcement."

The diners all gasped and then there was awed silence.

"No, no! Not that announcement!" the earl cried. "Not yet!"

Everyone exhaled in a whoosh and then laughed anxiously.

The earl cleared his throat. "Now that you are here, I wish to be certain we all understand why.

"Everyone 'round this table"—he gestured—"is here because he read my announcement in the papers."

An excited murmur rose and fell among the guests.

"Everyone who expressed a serious interest in the stone was invited."

That explained the rather egalitarian mix, I thought.

"As you know," the earl said, "I wish to make an announcement concerning the Instep Sapphire during the course of this house party, but I am not going to make that announcement just yet. I will be speaking with each of you about this matter in the coming days before I make my decision concerning the disposition of the stone."

"Disposition?" I asked. "Does that mean you will be selling the sapphire, Lord Instep? Will you be taking bids during the house party? Is that what this is about? For if so, I am honor-bound to inform the entire assemblage that, should I come into possession of the sapphire, I will gift my lovely bride with it, and as she is a treasure of great worth"—I cast a fond glance at Apple, who looked stunned—"I will be willing to pay a great price."

"So," old Countess Rangnor said, "You fared well in the Indies, ay Turnbull? Increased your fortunes?"

I laughed easily. "Fortunately for me, the gentlemen here in England like their tobacco and rum, and the ladies their chocolate and sugar."

Everyone laughed right along with us.

Someone else raised their hand to speak, and the questions flew fast and furious:

"Are you planning perhaps to give it to a good cause?" This from a hopeful vicar.

"Have you already made any preliminary decisions? Eliminated anyone from the running, perhaps?" This from an acknowleged scapegrace gambler.

"Will you be interviewing us to decide who is the most worthy?" This from Miss Ophelia Palin. "For if that is the case, I might as well pack my bags and hie back to London," she cackled.

"No need to be hasty," the earl smiled. "You will all know in good time," he said, "and, in the meantime, please do enjoy the house party. The grounds are extensive and you are welcome anywhere."

The earl was seated and someone drank his health, and as I raised my glass, I chanced a peek at Apple.

She was throwing me daggers. Big, sharp, jagged, poison-tipped daggers.

She'd finally figured it all out. She knew her supposed husband had a big sapphire in his pocket . . . and now she knew that sapphire was a fake—and that the fake husband was really a thief who wanted the real stone for himself!

CHAPTER THIRTEEN

Let me not to the marriage of true minds admit impediments!
—William Shakespeare

It was all I could do to sit through dinner without divesting my stomach of it. As soon as our host stood, signaling the end of the meal, I fled. Not to the parlor with the other ladies as was customary, leaving the gentlemen to their port, cigars, and chamberpots, but up the grand staircase and to the third floor, where I sought the safety and comfort of Constance's darkened bedchamber.

Opening the door, I slipped inside and sagged against the inside of the door, closing the lock with a satisfying *thunk*.

But I didn't really have a chance to relax before I noticed a still form in the bed and realized I hadn't even so much as looked at Constance all through supper.

She hadn't even been there!

"Oh, Constance are you quite all right?"

She nodded her head, which was mostly obscured by the covers.

"Tired?" I asked.

She hesitated a moment and then sighed, her voice cracking a little. The poor old dear. The last few days had been tiring even for me; I hadn't stopped to think how much more tiring they would be for a woman almost three times my age, though she hadn't seemed so very fatigued earlier in the day.

I stilled as another possibility occurred. Had Constance avoided supper because she knew what was going to happen? Had she known Posthumous was a thief and guessed that I would ferret out the truth at that first formal supper?

I could not believe that. Constance did not seem like such a coward. On the contrary, she seemed to take life by the horns, as it were.

There was only one way to find out.

"Posthumous is a thief!" I announced suddenly, watching for a reaction.

No response. That was odd.

"Did you hear me, Constance?" I asked. "Constance?"

Walking over to her side, I'd barely touched her when she sprang from the bed and past me, heading for the dressing room with a clattering and scuffling and slamming the dressing room door shut behind her.

Odd wasn't the word!

"Why is it so dark in here?"

"Ah . . . my lamp went out!" called a low, tremulous voice from the other side of the door.

"*Uncle John?* Is that you?"

"Uh . . . yes! I was . . . uh . . . waiting for you. I reckoned you would come here lookin' for Miss Cherry to help you change after dinner. Highborn ladies change after dinner, don't they?"

"How the blazes should I know?" I said irritably. "I am not a blasted viscountess! And neither is Mr. Jones!"

"Right glad I am you've noticed his gender at last!" Uncle said, coming into the room once more. He was wearing one of Posthumous's expensive gold-embroidered waistcoats, a scarlet satin dressing gown, a top hat, and no pants. I hardly took a second glance. "Was starting to wonder if"—he twirled one finger next to his temple—"if you were all quite there. A girl would have to be dicked in the nob to miss his charms, I should think."

I rolled my eyes. "Be serious, Uncle! What are we going to do?"

"I am serious! He's quite the gentleman. Why aren't you trying to snare him?"

I groaned and headed for the door. "I do not have time for such nonsense."

"I say, where are you going?"

"Straight to the earl. Posthumous Jones is a thief, and there is but one right course of action!"

Uncle moved with amazing speed, blocking my passage. "No! You mustn't," he warned.

"Why shouldn't I? He has lied to us from day one. He has lured us into a terribly dangerous situation! Do you realize that the moment he steals the earl's jewel, we will be considered his accomplices? We could be transported—or worse." I shuddered. "Turning him in is the only choice that makes sense! He is a thief. I can't see any reason to spare him! Can you?"

"What makes you think he hasn't already stolen the sapphire?"

"He *was* late to dinner . . ."

"He might have taken it then."

I thought about it for a moment and shook my head. "He hasn't taken it yet."

"How do you know?"

"If he had, he wouldn't be here still. He'd have flown."

Uncle John's face folded into lines of disapproval. "Would he?" he asked. "Would he leave you and me and Constance here?"

That moment will forever stick in my mind. A battle, a clash within me of heart against mind. Reason demanded I see black and white. Posthumous was a thief, and thieves were evil. But intuition demanded I recognize the shadows between black and white, between right and wrong: Posthumous was a kind, compassionate, fiercely loyal man. A good man.

How could a man be both good and evil?

Somehow guessing my struggle, Uncle tousled my hair. "That's right. Listen to your heart, my girl. What does it tell you?"

I gave him a rueful smile. "He would not leave us."

Uncle nodded. "I don't think so, either."

I sat wearily and sighed. "So I cannot tell the earl what Mr. Jones has planned. But I cannot just sit back and do nothing! I must stop him. I . . . I will take it from him," I said. "I will pick his pocket!"

Uncle John shook his head. "Dearest, you *are* a good sneak-thief. You have had to be with me around. But you are no pickpocket, and he is a great thief. That's why he caught you trying to put the sapphire back in his pocket to begin with."

As I buried my face in my hands, the mantel clock began to strike the hour. "What am I going to do?" I moaned.

"Ah . . . why not go to him and talk it over?" Uncle said, urging me to my feet and propelling me along. "Surely you shall be able to come to some sort of compromise." He opened the door.

"I don't want to face him!"

"You have to sometime, dearest. He *is* your husband, after all." He laughed—a little anxiously, I fancied—and glanced first at the clock and then down the hall, as though looking out for someone. "It is late. Run along, now." He gave me a gentle shove and clicked the door shut just as I caught a glimpse of the bed. Miss Cherry's bed.

It was covered with rose petals.

"So, the corn in your field is not cut until September?" I chattered away to the earl. Useless, polite conversation. Meaningless words people used only to fill the void of silence. We stood in the parlor after the meal, pass-

ing time as gentlemen did, I supposed. He was a pleasant enough companion, and I wondered what he would
be like if I got to know him. He seemed a good sort. A
good sort who would hate me, soon enough.

I was almost ashamed . . . but not quite.

As we stood there talking, Apple entered the parlor. She
had disappeared after supper, and I knew very well why.

"Mmm," I grunted, my attention focused now on Apple.
She looked lovely then, dressed in blue and white silk and
lace. Yet I longed to see her clothed in nothing but her
blushes.

An image of her lithesome, unblemished limbs floated
across my mind's eye—an image that, had it lingered a
second longer, would have awakened . . . parts of me I
wished to remain asleep.

I cleared my throat, and Leah's gaze swiveled in my
direction.

To my disbelief, she stared at me for half a heartbeat,
lifted her chin a notch, and then spun on her heels and
stalked out onto the terrace!

My beloved wife had delivered me the cut direct! In
public. And quite grandly. Grandly enough to elicit a few
hushed gasps from those who had witnessed the act.

Those gasps propelled me after her, but I took no more
than two steps before the earl stepped into my path, deliberately blocking my way, I immediately suspected.

I was right.

"I say . . . have you stuck your foot in it already, old man?
You are so newly wed for such troubles, I'd have thought!"

His remarks weren't unkindly delivered. I fancied he
was genuinely concerned. "No." I grasped for an easy lie.
"You know how women can be at times. She is simply in
need of some fresh air."

The earl sighed and nodded in understanding. "Yes, I
do remember . . ."

His hesitation gave me the opening I'd been looking

for all evening. "Your sapphire, it is a bauble meant to grace a woman's neck. How came you by it?"

The earl's gaze was drawn to his past as he said, "Many years ago I fell madly, wildly in love. Yes, you are correct. I purchased the gem for my lady, only to find out later she did not return my affection."

"I am sorry to hear that. That must have been a crushing blow."

The earl waved a hand in the air as if dismissing the pain radiating from his eyes. "I should have rid myself of the memory long ago. It was foolish of me to keep such a vivid reminder so close."

His pain was palpable, and I couldn't help an upwelling of genuine sympathy for the man as I asked, "That is why you seek to rid yourself of the gem now?"

He nodded. "Yes." His gaze darted toward the gardens before coming to rest once more upon me. "The sapphire would look lovely hanging at *your* lady's neck." One eyebrow rose as he added, "It glints beautifully in sunlight— almost as much as the light glinting off those daggers she was shooting you at dinner. My advice to you is that whatever you have done to offend her, you should apologize immediately—especially if it is not your fault."

"I have done nothing to offend her." *At least not in the last few minutes.*

The earl smiled a little sadly. "The love of a good woman is a precious thing, easy to let fall through a man's grasp."

"We did not marry for love."

"Ah, that may be true. But you spent two months on a ship together, did you not? Mark my words: she has fallen in love with you. Women who feel only apathy display only apathy. It takes real love to produce that much anger." He chuckled softly. "And those pretty words you spoke in the dining room earlier did not come from a man any less besotted. You love her just as much as she loves you, you lucky clod. So get out there before I throw you out there myself."

I didn't doubt that he would try it—and that he might just succeed. In his late fifties, the earl was still a strong, robust man. He was nearly my height and of similar build, but his eyes held a determination I'd rarely seen in other men, a bold resolve that matched my own.

"Yes sir." I gave a low bow and padded toward the tall, glass terrace doors.

"Good man." I heard him murmur behind me.

CHAPTER FOURTEEN

We are never deceived; we deceive ourselves.
—Johann Wolfgang von Goethe

I clutched the stone balustrade, my chin rising in defiance with every click of my false husband's approaching boot heels. I needn't turn to know Pos bore down on me. He would never allow such a snub to go unchallenged. Confusion rang through me, but I fought my conflicting emotions. I'd actually thought I loved him! How absurd.

The stinging in my eyes had everything to do with the wind sweeping across the terrace and nothing to do with caring for a thief who had played me for a fool. I would never allow myself to be used in such a nefarious scheme. If he couldn't find the strength of will to stop his plans, then I had to be strong enough for both of us.

At the last second, I turned and confronted my adversary, lifting a brow in silent inquiry, mostly for fear of my voice shaking if I tried to use it.

His gaze swept over me. "We need to talk."

Despite my feigned nonchalance, I felt an almost magnetic pull and wanted to step closer to him. Rubbish! "Sir," I said with pert formality, "I have no need to hear more of your lies."

"Apple—"

"Miss Grey," I corrected him. "And I shall refrain from calling you by *any* name, as I am no longer certain what your legal name is. But legalities are of minor importance to you, are they not?"

He stepped closer. "I am serious. This is not a game. You must listen to me."

Botheration, he was too handsome! I stepped back. "If you choose to tell me the truth, then perhaps I will listen." I turned to look over the earl's garden a dozen feet below the balustrade of the terrace. No escape there. Still, I was defiant. "Then again, perhaps not. Do you even remember how to tell the truth?"

He came up and stood behind me. Too close. So close I could feel the heat of his body sinking into mine. I could scarcely think and felt myself flush. "Back away," I ordered. "Now. People may be watching."

"Let them. We are married." He pressed into my skirts. "We've obviously quarreled, love. They all want us to make up."

"'Love' is it? How dare you? And I do not wish to make up. I want nothing more to do with you."

"The rapid pulse in your throat tells me a different story than the words from your lips, Apple." He slid his hands about my waist.

I turned and tried to push him away, but he barely moved. Instead, I set my jaw and looked him square in the eye. "Answer me this. Are you here to steal the earl's sapphire?" *Please say no.*

His eyes darkened. "Yes."

My hands trembled as I gripped the balustrade behind me, my voice as hard as the stone as I said, "Then you are a thief."

Posthumous laughed bitterly. "You say that as though there is nothing more offensive one could be. Oh, my dear Apple. How far I have fallen in your eyes! Yes, I am a thief, and, naturally, all thieves are bad. Is that correct?"

"Of course."

He leaned in closer, his arms trapping me as he clasped the rail on either side of me. "Have you not heard of honor among thieves? It does exist. Perhaps I am more honorable than you think. I haven't stolen your treasure. You have stolen my heart, but you are still a virgin."

"Stolen your heart? Nonsense!" But, even as I said it, blood rushed to my head, my heart pounded, and I leaned closer. He was so . . . alluring . . .

But at the last moment, even as I tried to block it, the memory returned. My mother's screams, my father's cries rose inside me, clawing at my regard, and I saw the highwaymen raise their pistols—

Shuddering, I pushed him away—with success this time—and met his gaze with new resolve.

"Thieves can have no honor," I repeated, hating the hurt that flared in his eyes. How dare he? He had no right to be hurt. I was the one who'd suffered damage.

"Shh!" He looked over his shoulder into the ballroom. "Do not let them hear you. They can tell we are arguing. Either kiss me or—Oh, never mind!" Taking my arm, he compelled me down the wide, curving steps and onto the garden pathway. The flagstones felt cold through my thin slippers.

I yanked my arm from his grasp as soon as we were out of sight of the ballroom. "You have systematically led me to believe you are something you are not. You are a fine actor as well as a thief. And I was taken in by your little game. But thievery is no game. It is wrong! People get hurt. They die."

"I don't hurt people and you know it."

"You threatened to kill those men at The Birdhouse!"

"With your approval, as I recall. Why can you not remember that now?"

"I thought you were someone else. Now I find I know nothing about you! You have heaped lie upon lie! You are a thief. You steal. Stealing is evil!"

"Fine. Tell yourself that. I am a thief. I steal. I am evil. What about your uncle? He steals all the time. Does that make him evil, too?"

"How many times must I say it? Uncle is not a thief. He-he just borrows things. He is like a child. He does not understand that what he does is wrong."

"He bloody well does understand!" Posthumous fumed. "Are you truly that naïve, or are you a hypocrite? Your uncle is one of the finest pickpockets I've ever seen!"

I slashed the air with my fist. "This conversation is over. We've made our respective opinions clear. I believe you are incorrect about my uncle. Stealing is wrong."

"Just like prostitution is wrong? And you never came to see another side of that picture."

I frowned, but didn't answer. His words tied me up in knots faster than I could untangle them.

"It must be so easy living in your world, Apple. Always knowing what to do. Everything laid out in black and white. Never a question. Never any confusion. Never a bloody gray area to make you wonder about a decision. Guilty. Not guilty."

"Sarcasm does not become you. And as much as you mean those comments as derision, for me they are a compliment to my steadfast nature. A nature I find quite comforting." I dropped my gaze. "Safety. Steadfastness. Responsible, honest, hardworking people find those things virtues. And so do I."

Posthumous tilted my chin up with one finger. "Safety, Apple? You sacrificed your own safety to protect your uncle."

"He is all I have left. The only one I . . . truly care about in my life."

Posthumous stiffened. "I see." He took a few steps away, and I thought he might leave, but he stopped and spoke again, without turning. "I admire your courage and loyalty. Your willingness to stand by and assist those who have helped you in the past."

"Do not attempt to flatter your way out of this. I suppose you already have the jewel and have hidden it by now."

He cocked his head. "What makes you say that?"

"You were late to dinner. I suppose you took it then."

He laughed. "You do think I am a scoundrel! The reason I was late was because I had an errand to attend to in the village. A very important and personal one, as it happens."

"Personal? What sort of errand could you possibly have in Maddermark village?"

"There is a family there. The mother is widowed, and she has a sick little girl."

Concern warred with curiosity. "How do you know that?"

"I have been here before. I visit them whenever I pass through Maddermark."

"Oh?" I quelled a sudden urge to rip a certain widow's hair from her head. "You often pass through here and . . . ah . . . visit?"

"I often pass through many villages. I . . . do not have a home. I have spent my life traveling from place to place. I know many people, and sometimes I help them."

"Stealing from the rich and giving to the poor? Do you fancy yourself another Robin Hood?"

A dark flush seared his face. "Not so noble as he."

It wasn't a hum. His voice made that clear, and I watched a rapid parade of emotions shape his features—first anger, then disgust, then sadness, none of it directed at me, but at himself! It was a rare, unguarded moment, gone in the space of two heartbeats.

Stunned, I looked away. Never in the eight years I'd known him had I seen him anything but confident and malapert. What did it mean? And what did it mean that he had allowed me to see it? Was the display a mistake or a deliberate act?"

He looked . . . lost. Alone. So achingly alone.

I stared at the stars, trying to make sense of it all and

failed. And so my next words came not from my head but from my confused heart: "Then . . . that was a good thing you did. How can you do such lovely things and still be a thief?"

I walked to his side and touched his sleeve. "What are you?" I whispered. "Who are you? Hero or villain?"

Turning, he captured my hand in his and held it captive. "I am no hero, but neither am I evil, Apple. I swear it."

Troubled, I pulled my hand away.

He let me go and then raked his fingers through his dark hair. "Back to those damn shades of gray again, Apple?" He sighed. "You are so wrong. Nothing in this world is black and white."

All at once, an idea sprang into my mind fully formed. Did I dare go through with it? "*You* are wrong," I said. "Some things are black or white."

"Name one thing."

I looked up at him through my lashes. "My desire to kiss you. No shades of gray there."

He blinked and then exhaled, closing his eyes, and I thought for a moment he'd seen through the half-lie, but then in one smooth movement, he pulled me into his arms with a low growl and . . . and he ravished me. There is simply no other description.

His lips came down on mine, hot, firm, and possessive as if he'd waited through all of time to claim me. I don't know how long it lasted. Reason, logic, practicality—they all spun away. The world might have spun off its axis and crashed into the moon along with them, and I wouldn't have noticed. Nothing mattered but him. The press of his body against mine. The way his fingers slid into my hair to hold me still for his kiss. And the kiss! It went on and on, urgent, then tender, then deep, then soft. He was a sorcerer, wielding a magic both wild . . . and gentle.

It took me a moment to register that he'd let me go. And when my eyes fluttered open, he wore the hint of a knowing grin.

"More than you bargained for, Apple?"

"Mmm . . ." I murmured, "more . . . I definitely want more."

"As you wish!" And he kissed me again.

I let him. He was going to steal the earl's sapphire, and I was going to help him.

And then I was going to save him from himself!

CHAPTER FIFTEEN

Do not count your chickens before they are hatched.
                                        —Aesop

It wasn't stealing if you stole something from a thief and gave it back to its owner. Was it?

I twisted the hem of my nightrail and tried to calm myself. For three days and nights, as we carried out our plan, I had behaved as a solicitous wife in public and as a concerned and contrite lover in private. To my relief—and confusion—Posthumous Jones had continued to be a gentleman, in spite of my apparent change of heart toward him. Oh, he'd continued to issue roguish invitations, but he'd laughed when I refused, when he might have pressed me for a more physically sincere response. He was actually honoring my maidenly honesty! How much more angry would Posthumous be when he found out what I intended to do to him!

My nerves were strung as tight as bowstrings that night. I was going to help him steal the Instep Sapphire!

La, how I wished he would stop watching me! I could feel the marks of guilt written all over my face. Unlike everyone else around me, it seemed, I was not a consummate liar, and if he learned I planned to hide the stone and send a note for the earl disclosing its location, he would be angry beyond belief—and I couldn't blame him!

I turned to face him now. "Honestly. I do not see why you cannot trust me. I told you I would help you switch sapphires."

"Yes. You did."

I picked up a pillow and threw it in what I hoped was a convincing display of frustration. "Then what *is* the trouble? You have everything you wanted. I have agreed to your fantastic scheme. Why are you still questioning my motives?"

He leaned against the doorjamb, watching. Watching, always watching. That was Posthumous Jones. That had been Posthumous Jones from the day we'd met!

"Why?" he drawled. "Because I'm not sure why you changed your mind. Did my amazing powers of persuasion finally convince you that you suddenly needed to pursue a life of crime? Or did you need more excitement in your life?"

I walked around the bed, smoothing out invisible wrinkles—anything to avoid looking Posthumous in the eye. Anything to keep him from catching me in a lie. "Don't be silly," I said with a coy glance up through my lashes. "Your . . . your kiss was enough excitement to last for a lifetime—or hours, at least."

With gratitude, I noted that my comment had derailed his train of thought. But, of course, I hadn't planned much beyond that and soon found myself cornered near the headboard of the four poster.

Reaching beyond me, he lazily grasped the carved wooden post, effectively cutting off my escape—not that I dared try. "Hours, hmm? Are you in need of a restorative dose, perhaps?"

He leaned down and his lips caught mine once more. La, the man could kiss! Just as I was about to turn into an addlepated twit once more, I realized his thoughts may have been derailed, but his steam engine was in complete working order. If I didn't start thinking clearly soon, the sapphire wouldn't be the only jewel stolen this evening!

Breathing heavily, I pushed against him, biting my lip and fighting the urge to linger there with my hands pressed on the wide expanse of his chest. This was not going as I'd expected. I certainly hadn't expected to like kissing him. Like? Adore is more the word. Kissing is definitely underrated. At least when one is kissing Posthumous Jones!

"Do you not think we should go do whatever it is thieves do at this time of night?" I asked. Even to my own ears my voice sounded breathless.

"Call me Pos, Apple. When a lady has been kissed as thoroughly as you have, formality is rather comical."

"Very well. What exactly is your master plan, Pos? Do we blacken our faces? Dress in dark clothes and skulk about?"

Sighing in obvious resignation that no more kisses were forthcoming, he draped himself across the bed and, with a last vestige of hope, patted the counterpane beside him in invitation.

I rolled my eyes and went to sit on the far side of the room.

"Ah, my dear brave Apple," he laughed. "You shall have to garner more courage than that for our venture tonight," he finished, running his palm over the counterpane in slow, circular motions as if caressing a lover's skin. I watched, paralyzed, feeling my own skin begin to heat. I'd never really noticed what strong, masculine hands he—

"The plan," he said, yanking my rogue attention from his hands, "is to walk straight up to the sapphire, grab it, put our fake in its place, and walk out."

It took a moment for his words to sink into my ridiculously distracted brain. "Are you daft? The sapphire rests on a raised dais in an empty ballroom, guarded by two gargantuan men with no sense of humor that I have detected!"

"Ah, but you've said the magic word: men. *They are men.* Specifically, two men for whom the last two weeks have been incredibly lonely."

I straightened my spine. "You had best not be thinking—"

"No!" He sat up, his own indignation flaring. "Bloody hell, give me *some* credit for decency, Apple, will you? I would never. Surely you know me better than that?"

Mollified, I relaxed. "Sorry. I think. Tell me more."

"We were discussing the guards."

"The *lonely* guards," I stressed.

"Yes, the terribly lonely, *faithful* guards that the earl has posted on sapphire watch tonight. I have learned that the one poor devil's wife has provided him with nine offspring and twenty-two grandchildren. The other is awaiting the birth of his first and is as nervous as a fox when the hounds are loosed."

"What does this have to do with anything?"

"The guards feel most solicitously toward you, my dear wife. You are in such a delicate condition!" He rose from the bed and took my hand, bowing over it and sweeping a kiss across my knuckles. "If you should happen to swoon again, fair lady—while these guards are present, of course—they would surely come to your rescue. Even if only for a fleeting moment."

"Are you saying . . . ?"

Posthumous Jones smiled a roguish smile that made my toes curl. "The way to the earl's sapphire is through your 'vapors,' my dear. Make them dramatic, and make them last."

My dear little accomplice looked convincingly pale in the flickering light of the wall sconces as we made our way down the wide hallway toward the main staircase. Few were about at this late hour, but a nocturnal visit to the kitchen to satisfy the strange cravings of my wife's condition would not have been too far-fetched.

"I am going to be sick, and I will not have to pretend a swoon."

"Just opening-night jitters," I said, sliding my arm about Apple's waist and drawing her closer. "You'll be fine."

I could feel her shaking increase with each step nearer our destination. "Buck up, love. Surely a woman who can withstand the courtly advances of a dashing town buck such as Portman Lowell should be able to postpone her collapse until a more opportune moment."

She shot me a glare that could have leveled mountains to mere rubble, then pushed away from me to stalk forward in a huff.

Much better. Now her nerves wouldn't give us away. Although her spring down the stairs might garner some unwanted attention. "Steady, love. This is not the derby! Timing is everything. A lady descends the stairs with grace and dignity."

"And how does a dastard descend if he's knocked on his—"

I grabbed her and claimed her lips—the best way I could think of to quiet the feisty termagant. God, I loved her . . . I loved every blessed thing—

Shock slammed into my chest like a cannonball, my hands dropped to my sides, and I stared at her, shaken. It wasn't true. I couldn't let it be.

Concern replaced the anger in Apple's expression. "What is it? What is wrong?"

"Nothing. Nothing that time can't fix."

"Time?"

"Twenty minutes. Which is about as long as I think it will take for us to take the gem and be back in our bedchamber. Together. Alone." I waggled my eyebrows, forced something that I hoped passed as a grin onto my face, and continued down the hall—but for the first time, I questioned what I was doing. Who I was. What I was asking her to become.

Blast. What was I thinking? The chit had me all twisted inside.

I'd been a lad. I hadn't had a choice but to steal. And I'd stopped stealing as soon as I could. Given every dime I had ever since to atone for my actions. And now I wasn't stealing at all. I was righting a wrong. A grave wrong.

The sapphire had been stolen from me along with my mother and my childhood. It was ridiculous to waver because of some self-righteous black-and-white spinster.

Sliding my hand into my pocket, I fingered the gold medallion. I would never get a chance like this again, and I knew it. The gem had lain hidden all these years, and now that it had surfaced, I had to take it before it changed hands, else it might go to ground again. I had learned the hard way that life seldom offers second chances.

We went by the kitchen, as we had done for the past two nights, where I raided the larder for my wife to satisfy her odd cravings. The night kitchen maid was used to helping me stow a sickening array of food into a basket, ostensibly to take back to our room. This time it was dewberry tarts, cold chicken, cucumber pickles, pineapple, a crock of stewed eels, and milk in a wicker basket.

We strolled past drawing rooms and salons, extending greetings to the few other late-night prowlers for whom final games of chance or piquet had not whetted the appetite for sleep. At last, we came to the ballroom. Our final destination for the last several nights.

"Uh-oh," I muttered as we neared the ballroom, for the soft sounds of a harpsichord wafted through the open, ornately carved, gilt double doors as we neared. At the far end, away from the stalwart guards who flanked the sapphire perched on its white velvet-draped pillar of white marble, a lone figure wearing a black garb and veil coaxed the lilting music from the instrument, the melody both beautiful and haunting. Mrs. Mapes, the strange woman Leah had befriended.

Apple's eye's lit with excitement! "She is playing a waltz!" she whispered so as not to disturb Mrs. Mapes.

My heart did a strange patter in my chest, and I chuckled. It wasn't a show. "Utterly scandalous. Do I dare hold you in public?"

"Scandal has not troubled you thus far."

"Then shall we dance, my dear viscountess?" I put the basket down on the wooden floor.

She bit her lip. "I have never danced with anyone but the girls at The Maiden," she hissed. "And then we were only just having a bit of fun."

I held out my arms to her. "Do you trust me?" I held my breath waiting for her answer. Somehow, my question—and her answer—raised a deep longing, which I buried immediately.

Leah hesitated a moment, then put her hand in mine. I slid my arm around her waist and pulled her close. Too close. She knew it, and I waited for her to protest, but I met her gaze, let her see the full power of my need for her in my eyes, and the words died on her lips.

We danced, slowly at first, circling the ballroom, but the music didn't end. Mrs. Mapes looked over her shoulder, smiled, and one melody transformed into another and then another.

We danced until the faintest sheen of sweat gleaned on Apple's skin. Her face was flushed. Tendrils of hair flew free of their confines. She leaned toward me and stretched, lifting her lips to mine.

How I wanted to free her of the confines of her life! To taste the salt upon her skin. To make the flush of the dance be the more florid flush of—

"Do you have the fake?" she whispered.

I was obviously losing my touch—or my mind. "I have been mentally disrobing you in preparation for ravishment," I whispered back, "while you have been thinking only of the sapphire!" I laughed, unable to help myself. "You wound my ego, my dear. I was trying to be seductive."

"And you have been succeeding for nigh on a quarter hour!" she said crossly. "The ever-faithful guards are going to question how a delicate pregnant woman capable of tromping multiple circuits around a massive ballroom with her seductive husband suddenly gets the vapors while standing perfectly still looking at a shiny blue rock. Be serious. After this, I look healthy enough to run the Derby with you riding me!"

"Mmm . . ." I murmured. "An image that bears closer examination."

"Later," she snapped. "It is time we get on with this production."

"Then get ready for your swoon, darling, because this is your grand finale." With that, I twirled and whirled and whisked and swirled her until the flush on her face was replaced by a quite convincing shade of green.

"Stop! I am going to fai—"

"Precisely, darling."

My last flourish had her coming to a dazed stop just before our much amused guards, while I was off to one side of them. Leah took one look at the two men and her eyes slowly rolled back in her head. Both men had jumped forward to catch her—and the sapphire was switched— before she ever touched the floor. It was an incredibly convincing performance.

My lord, I loved the woman! She was spectacular. Daring. Brave. Brazen, even!

And unconscious?

Damnation, she wasn't faking!

The music stopped abruptly. "My lord," Mrs. Mapes said, "I think you should take your lady to her room and skip your nightly picnic. Both of you have had enough *excitement* for one evening."

The emphasis on the word "excitement" chilled me to the bone. I raised my gaze to meet her veiled gaze. Had she seen me switch the sapphire? I'd been careful to make sure her view was blocked. Still, if she'd seen something, surely she would have exposed me forthwith! Wouldn't she?

She would, I decided, and then a soft moan drew my attention.

"What happened? Did you—?"

"Catch you? No, darling. I am afraid that honor went to these two fine gentlemen." I turned to the men. "Please, tell me your names."

The two guards exchanged glances, unsure if they were in trouble or not. The older guard said, "Me name's Beauregard. After me Da."

The young man's face reddened. "I only have one name. Thompson, milord."

"Beauregard. Thompson. I can never thank you enough. You have saved my wife from a hard fall onto a wooden floor. In her delicate condition, you might very well have saved the family line! I can never repay you! Beauregard and Thompson. I think we could fit those two names into our family register when our son is born. What do you think, dearest?"

Amid the protests and delight of the guards, my lovely Apple just smiled. "I think, my lord, that you are one of the most astounding men I have ever met."

Mrs. Mapes looked askance at the two of us. "I think, perhaps, you are right about that!" she said.

When we returned to our chamber, Posthumous made a beeline for the lamp and lit it before pulling a loupe from his pocket and peering at the stone. "You were marvelous, my dear! You fainted beautifully."

"I fainted convincingly because I fainted!"

"Sorry about that." He laughed with no conviction, which vexed me. "I know you were a bit tight-strung. I should have been more careful." Sighing, he put the stone in a valise and began to undress.

"Anything wrong?"

"No," he said. "I am just . . . relieved. That is all."

"So our adventure here is over?"

"It will be tomorrow at first light. You will be ill—which dovetails nicely with your swoon!—and you will require our immediate removal to London, where we will be seeking the best physician for you and our child."

"I see."

He took his time undressing and then coming to bed. I don't know if he bothered to wear anything to bed, for I pretended to already be fast asleep. In spite of my persistent curiosity I did not peek as he emerged from the dressing room—eyes shut, eyes shut, eyes shut!—and by supreme force of will I moved not a muscle as he slid into bed beside me and softly whispered, "Awake, Apple?"

Seconds passed, and finally he sighed and subsided against his pillow and was still.

I waited until the clock struck the hour of two and then three, just to be sure, and then I slipped carefully, soundlessly out of bed and padded across the floor to the washstand. After moistening an edge of my wrapper with water from the ewer, I crept to the dressing room door and used the water to lubricate the hinges. A telltale squeak would have been disastrous!

That accomplished, I opened the door inch by painful inch and stole into the dressing room, and closed the door again before finding his valise—unlocked, thank goodness, for Uncle's tutoring had stopped at picking pockets, and I had no way of knowing if his skills ran to picking locks!

I slipped the sapphire from the valise and lit a candle before waking Uncle, who was snoring softly on his cot in the dressing room.

"Uncle!" I whispered, shaking him awake. "Uncle!"

"Mm?"

"Shh!"

"Mm?"

"Shh! Make no sound!"

Wiping the sleep from his eyes, he sat up and whispered back. "What is it?"

I held out the candle and the sapphire. "I took it from him."

"You stole it?" A delighted smile blossomed on his face. "From Mr. Jones?"

"I did not steal it. I am merely returning it to its rightful owner!"

"Oh!"

"I need your help."

"Certainly, certainly. Of course." He yawned.

"I need you to hide the stone until after we leave."

"Hide it? Hide it where? Why?"

"Somewhere on the estate, somewhere safe yet easily found again. I intend to write anonymously to the earl after we are gone to tell him where to find the sapphire."

Uncle nodded happily. "Clever." He stood. "Just a moment." Imagine my astonishment as Uncle reached into Posthumous's valise, drawing forth the loupe in seconds without even looking! My mouth must have been hanging open, for he grinned. "Practice," he said. "I have nimble, knowing fingers."

I heaved a sigh as he opened the loupe and held it up to the candle. I must have been weary, for I didn't stop to question what he was doing before he flicked the loupe closed.

"A fake," he pronounced.

"What?"

"It is a fake. A faux. A counterfeit, a—"

"I know what it means! What do *you* mean?"

"I pinched the real sapphire before you got to it and switched it for Mr. Jones's fake without him knowing it," he said with obvious glee.

I sat with a *flump* onto Uncle's cot. We had just "stolen"

a fake sapphire, when we'd had the real one in our hand all along.

"Why would you do such a thing?"

"Couldn't have him stealing it now, could we?" He chuckled softly and shook his head. "Took it right out of his pocket! That'll teach the lad to go thinking he's a better thief than I am!"

"*You are* not *a thief!*"

"Yes, I am! And a very good one! The Blackbird, they called me—always left behind a black feather, you see—blending into the night and leaving no trace to follow, not even a shadow, like I'd simply flown away."

The room tilted. "You? A common thief?" I murmured.

"Oho! A common thief? Some pickpocket or cutpurse? No! I was a professional. A hired thief. The best. I was better than the Peacock. Still am," he said with a jaunty wink.

"The Peacock?"

"The brazen rogue took to leaving a peacock feather behind when he was hardly more than a lad! A blatant imitation of me—an open challenge!—and every thief in the land knew it." There was no ire in his voice, only a chuckle. "Truth to tell, I was flattered."

Burying my face in my hands, I tried to make sense of it all but felt like my head might burst. Darling Uncle . . . a thief? Dear Uncle, sweet, loving, dotty Uncle . . . had been some sort of master thief? And that Posthumous Jones still was? The two men I loved the most in the whole world were both scoundrels? The room tilted some more. I clutched the seat of my chair and tried not to be ill.

"Wasn't sure until a year or so ago. I'd had my suspicions for months, and then one day he'd stopped at The Maiden as usual, and I saw a feather peeking out from his valise—three guesses as to what sort of feather it was—and it's then I knew. And I started to plan."

"For what?"

He smiled. "For your future. I'll be gone someday."

"I know, Uncle, and you have my wholehearted blessing, really you do."

"Well! I knew you'd take the news that I'm a thief badly, but I didn't think you'd wish me dead!"

"Dead! Aren't you talking about marrying Miss Cherry?"

"Oh!" He laughed. "That. Would if I could, but she won't have me. I asked her years ago."

"Years ago?"

"Yes. I, ah . . . met Constance a few years before you were born. Traveling is a necessity in my profession, you see—gave it up to be with you when you lost your parents."

"Why did you not tell me you knew her?"

"Well, it is not the sort of thing one talks about, now is it?"

"Oh." I felt my eyes go wide. "Oh! You mean . . . you and Constance—*Oh!*"

He cleared his throat and worried the rim of his hat. "It isn't like that. She wasn't a working girl. I visited The Birdhouse once or twice, but then I ended up falling in love—with *her*! I asked her to marry me," he said, "but she had her young ladies to take care of, and then I had you. Couldn't very well move a fourteen-year-old girl into The Birdhouse. And so she . . . she refused me." And then he shed a tear. Uncle, who was always merry, always cheerful. Dashing at his eye, he sniffled and then mumbled, "Sorry."

"Oh, Uncle!" I knelt and took his hands in mine, forgetting he'd just confessed to being a thief. "You have nothing to be sorry for. How dreadful for you that must have been! I am the one who should be apologizing. Because of me, you and Constance were forced to sacrifice your own happiness!"

"Not your fault, my dear, not your fault! I have enjoyed watching you grow. You are an extraordinary young lady. And a good sneak-thief!" He chuckled, regaining some balance. "You had to be! I made sure of that."

"I do not understand."

"Did you not wonder why I borrowed things? There ain't many opportunities in this world for ladies. Pinching things is something to fall back on. Something to keep the wolves from the doorstep, as it were. Something to keep your belly full and your back dry in time of need."

"La! Uncle! All those years, you were training me to be a thief?"

"Indeed! Did a good job of it, too, if I do say so myself—and I do," he added with a chuckle. "No reason not to beat my own drum a little. You turned out well. Worthy of a duck feather at least!"

"Uncle! How can you think that? I would never steal!"

"Never?" He looked at me shrewdly. "Haven't you already stolen from Posthumous, dearling?"

I covered my face with my hands. "That is what *he* said!" I stifled a heaving sob and began to cry.

"Now, now! None of that. This is hardly a time for tears. All will be well. Love is in the air! Soon, I will be wed to Constance and you will be wed to Mr. Jones, and we shall all be one family. One very happy family. Of course, we shall live at The Birdhouse and you at The Maiden, but—or perhaps not; I fancy Mr. Jones has quite a large nest egg stashed away somewhere."

The world tilted some more—upside down now, for my stomach dropped into my throat.

"You want me to marry Posthumous Jones?" I managed to rasp out.

"Why of course, dearling! You are perfect for each other. You shall be so happy together. We shall all be happy."

"You are mistaken! I do not love Posthumous Jones! He is a thief!"

His face crumpled. "Oh." He stood. "Well then." He turned his back to me. "I shall inform Constance in the morning. She was looking forward to a Christmas wedding."

"You have asked her to marry you?"

"No." Uncle shook his head. "Not formally, at least. But

we had spoken of it. At our age, one cannot wait for formalities." He opened the door. "I am tired, Leah. Do you mind?" He gestured toward the hall. It was a clear dismissal, and it was the first one he'd ever issued to me.

"Why can you not marry Constance?"

"Before your mother died, she lay in my arms and begged me to take care of you. I promised her I would, and I will. I had thought that finding you a good husband would fulfill that obligation, but you do not like my choice, so . . . that, as you often say, is that." He smiled tremulously.

Dazed and confused and feeling a crushing grief and guilt, I swerved down the hall, my eyes misting over with tears. Pausing at a corner, I slumped against the wall with my eyes closed.

And that is how Portman Lowell found me.

CHAPTER SIXTEEN

When my love swears that she is made of truth, I do not be-lieve her, though I know she lies.

—William Shakespeare

What are you doing here?

I pulled the question back from my lips just in time. I wasn't supposed to know him.

He came down the hall, staring down his nose in my direction. "I say, what goes here?"

I was red-eyed, dazed, surely rumpled, and slumping against a wall—a mull. Any fool could see that, and Mr. Stinky wasn't a fool, unfortunately. Thankfully, he looked beyond me, not directly *at* me. The cut, intentional or not, might have insulted me at one time, but now I was grateful for his impersonal attention.

Straightening my spine, I brushed at the skirt of my dress. "La, nothing but an over-tiring day. I am in need of some fresh air." To ascertain whether he recognized me or not, I inquired in the most imperious tone I could muster at the moment, "And why are you roaming the halls at this hour, Mr . . . ?"

His nose pointed higher. "Mr. Portman Lowell, a guest of the earl's. One of my horses had the temerity to die on

my way here, and the carriage overturned—though I
was unhurt, thank goodness. It took the longest three days
of my life waiting for the repairs to be finished."

I could do little but gasp. Not at the troubles he'd
faced, but at the callousness ringing so loudly in his tone
of voice.

He eyed me without eyeing me. "We have met before, I
think." He deigned to grace me with a slight bow. "And you
are . . . ?"

Unable to tell if he toyed with me or not, I stayed true
to my designated course. "Lady Turnbull."

That gained his attention. Before, I'd been but the Viscount Turnbull's "lady fair." Now I was his lady wife. Mr.
Stinky's nose lowered to a more personable level. "Ah, my
pleasure. You are here for the sapphire?"

I tipped my head and shrugged. "Are we all not here
for the same purpose?" A tiny voice inside my head
laughed at my question. No, we were not all here for the
same purpose. Some wanted to gain the gem legally,
while others . . .

"Yes, yes we are. I pray I am not too late."

"Here you are, here we are still, and so is the sapphire."

"Obviously. And my arrival means the rest of you are
here for no good purpose."

I stepped back. "I beg your pardon?" It was hard to keep
the overt sarcasm out of my tone, but I gave it my best.
"You think the sapphire is already yours?"

"Most definitely. The sapphire and"—he airily motioned across the room with a limp wave of a hand—"all
else. The earl is without an heir." Mr. Stinky tossed his
head before adding, "I am a distant cousin. The courts
will take their time sorting out who is first in line, but eventually they will discover that it is me."

"You sound certain of that."

"I am. I assure you, my research is flawless." He stared
down at me. "So . . . Lady Turnbull . . . you grew up in
Boston?"

His slight hesitation set my heart to flutter. Was he toying with me? "Yes," I answered in what I hoped was a strong voice. "I did."

A deep, prolonged frown crossed Mr. Stinky's brow. "But you do not speak with much of a colonial accent."

I raised my own eyebrows in the haughtiest manner I could muster. "The society I kept is most civilized." After piercing him with a stare, I asked, "Have you been to the colonies, Mr. Lowell?" Fighting a sigh at his negative response, I informed him, "It is quite the same as it is here. We dress the same, eat the same things, and speak the same way."

What could only be described as a wicked smirk crossed his mouth. "And you wear the same jewelry, I see."

Before I knew what he was about, he bent low, grasped my fingers and brushed his thin lips across the back of my hand. His lingering touch turned my stomach. His touch was far too familiar and far too unwelcome. For all he knew, I was a married lady and we were alone in a deserted, darkened hallway. With a sharp gasp, I snatched my hand back and graced him with my most daunting glare.

"I may have grown up in a savage land, sir, but even I recognize that was most improper!"

He immediately appeared quite contrite and stepped away. "Forgive me, Lady Turnbull. You are quite right." And with a bob of his head, he marched off.

I stared after him, speechless, my heart threatening to beat its way out of my chest, and sagged against the wall once more. Portman Lowell—one of the guests? How? I tightly closed my eyes, fighting off a threatening headache, pinched the bridge of my nose, and moaned softly. Could this miserable adventure possibly get any worse?

Yes! my inner voice shouted. *It can!*

Mr. Lowell might have recognized me. I tried to calm myself. It appeared my clothing, manner, false name, and seven years had fooled him once again. He'd not even remarked on a resemblance to anyone from his past.

I inhaled deeply, then exhaled, trying desperately to relax. My deception was safe—for now. Everything was going to be fine.

It had to be.

"Hold on a minute, Stephanie." Erma opened a third volume and drew forth an old, brown-stained envelope. "Here," she said, handing it to Kristen. "Read this."

Kristen opened the letter carefully:

> *"Dear Mr. Perkins,*
>   *As a subject of the crown I feel a Certain Responsibility to preserve and protect the rights and privileges of the aristocracy, may those noble and faithful worthies ever flourish! As such, it has come to my attention that a certain Lady may not be deserving of the privileges appertaining to her Assumed station, and I urge you to ascertain the facts at your earliest convenience and before the close of the Earl of Instep's house party a week hence. Thank you for your swift attention and I remain*
>   *Your faithful servant and etc.,*
>   *Mr. Portman Lowell, esq. "*

All the younger ladies gasped.

"Crap!" Tamera slapped the arm of the chair. "They're in trouble now!"

"Gee, ya think?" Amy said with a sarcastic lift of her shoulders. "Man, I'd like to kick that dweeb where the sun don't shine!"

All of the girls laughed, and the mantel clock chimed the hour.

"One in the morning!" Allison said. "Quick, Steph, start reading again before Erma shuts us down!"

They all laughed again as Erma smiled indulgently and Stephanie eagerly complied:

Posthumous was awake when I came back into the room.

"I wondered why you had agreed to help me," he said. "And now I know. You were trying to stop me from stealing the gem. You are clever."

"So are you."

"Is stealing always wrong? No matter the reason?"

"Yes."

"And is lying always wrong?"

"Yes."

"No matter the reason?"

"Yes."

"Well, then, Apple, you are as unethical as I am, for you stole the sapphire from me!"

"I was simply returning it to its rightful owner. That is not stealing. Besides . . . what I took from you was a fake!"

"Do I detect the faint blush of a triumphant smile, Apple?" He laughed.

"What do you find so humorous, you impossible man?"

"I knew it was a fake. Why else would I have gone to sleep and left it unprotected? Think you I am that stupid?"

"Yes."

"Liar."

I said not another word, but pulled three cowbells from my own valise, tying one to the window and one to each door.

He watched with a smile. It was obvious what I was doing; the bells would wake me if he tried to leave in the middle of the night.

"What will the servants think, Apple?"

"That I don't trust you to stay in bed at night."

I slid into bed, and spent the next hour smelling him and listening to him.

Bother!

"Leah," he said, just before I fell asleep from sheer exhaustion.

"Yes?"

"Neither of us has been lying whenever we have kissed."

No. We hadn't been. And that is what bothered me the most.

I awakened the next morning with Apple in my arms, our legs and arms entwined. I lay still for the space of thirty seconds and, immediately, I knew she was only pretending to be asleep. I "awakened" her with a soft kiss and then abandoned the bed.

She avoided me the entire day.

The earl gave a ball that night, but I'd not danced once in the first hour. Apple was steadfastly avoiding my gaze, and I'd decided to just let her be. She had been avoiding looking at me all that day.

Somewhere after midnight, while talking to the earl, I cast a fleeting glance at Apple. How pretty she was! Blue suited her. Her new gowns were much closer-fitting than anything I'd seen her in back at The Dancing Maiden. She was as well turned out as any tonnish lady, and it was difficult to believe she belonged more in a taproom than a ballroom.

The earl caught me staring.

"So, is it true you have nineteen spaniels?" he asked.

"Mmm."

"And a herd of elephants?"

"Mmm," I murmured again, unhearing.

When he laughed, I realized what he'd said. "I beg your pardon, Instep. I am not myself tonight."

He nodded toward Leah. "She isn't either."

"Oh?"

"She has been avoiding your eyes all day."

I was saved of the necessity of framing some sort of reply by the appearance of an Arabian prince in the ballroom.

He was wearing orange brocade shoes curled in an upward spiral at the toe, which was adorned with a golden tassel. He had orange trousers, a scarlet coat that exposed his belly above his navel—which was covered by a royal blue satin girdle with silver bells attached that jingled when he walked—and to top it all off, a huge, purple, faux-bejeweled turban.

Several people snickered. One or two pointed. Deaf old Countess Ragnor, with a look of disgust on her face, cried in a whisper-that-was-not-a-whisper, "His turban is prettier than mine!"

I covered my face with my hand. "Please tell me my valet is not dressed as a pasha."

The earl laughed. "You're lucky he didn't dress as Cleopatra."

"Cleopatra?"

"Did you not know? Your valet has been . . . somewhat entertaining today. My mother loved masquerade balls, you see, and many of her costumes are still tucked away up in the trunks in the garrets. Apparently"—he nodded toward Mr. Bird—"he found them."

"My apologies. I shall take care of this forthwith."

"No, no, no! Please, let him stay. He is harmless and . . . rather amusing."

I watched as John bowed to Constance, almost losing that outrageous turban, and asked her for a dance. Constance, for her part, smiled regally and took his arm. They joined the set of dancers as though nothing untoward were happening, while the rest of the guests, taking their cues from the earl, looked on with indulgent smiles.

"I thank you for your indulgence," I said to the earl. "He has always been a good man."

"Have you known him long?"

I nodded. "Since God wore nappies."

He smiled. "I understand. My old nurse was living in

the nursery and still telling me to tuck in my shirt in her nineties. Never could understand how some people can dismiss servants. We have always taken care of ours. Like you, it seems."

"What about *your* hounds?" I asked, wishing to change the subject. It worked. The earl was a great lover of animals and loved to talk about his dogs. As it happened, I didn't have to feign interest in his hounds, for though I'd never lived in one place long enough to own one, I liked dogs, too. I can remember when I was young, watching other boys cavorting with their dogs and wishing I could have one of my own. But I could hardly feed myself sometimes and knew I had no business owning a dog I could not take care of. Even now, I looked forward to the day when I would settle somewhere. The first order of business would be to find a puppy or two. Maybe a whole litter.

As the earl talked, I glanced at Apple once again.

She was ensconced in a corner, talking animatedly with three much older ladies, and appeared to be enjoying herself. She hadn't looked in my direction once, which was probably not a bad thing, for then she could not see me staring at the sapphire.

It had been in my grasp—or so I had thought. And then Mr. Bird switched the thing. Picked my pocket for the fake and switched it for the real thing. I'd had it right in my pocket for two days!

Now, once more—courtesy of Leah and me!—the earl had the stone on display right there in the ballroom. A ballroom that was nicely crowded.

I smiled. A crowd was a thief's best friend.

Out of the corner of my eye, I saw Posthumous smile and wondered why. With that crush of guests, he had no chance to steal the gem. It was no matter. For now, the sapphire was safe, and for the first time that day, I was able to relax. Mrs. Mapes had introduced me to Miss

Ophelia Palin and Lady Griselda Waring, a pair of old
friends who, though unacquainted with Mrs. Mapes
before the house party, seemed to dovetail nicely with her
personality. They were a little older than she, but they were
both as kind, garrulous, and amiable as she was, and we
chatted companionably on a variety of subjects—though
I did have to steer quite vigorously away from talk of the
Viscountess Turnbull's personal life. Which was difficult,
as Miss Palin, particularly, seemed quite curious, though
she politely subsided once I'd made it clear that I was uncomfortable speaking of myself.

After a while, Mrs. Mapes excused herself and went in
search of the ladies' retiring room—a lovely luxury, that;
no more chill, drafty trips to the necessary in the middle
of the night!—and Lady Griselda asked, "Why does she
want the gem?"

"Have you seen the locket she wears?" Miss Palin asked.
I nodded. "It holds a miniature of her daughter."

Lady Griselda nodded. "I have seen it, too. Pretty girl.
Sapphire, they called her, for her eyes."

"They were a magnificent shade," Miss Palin agreed.

"But what has that to do with the gem?"

I said nothing, not wishing to betray a confidence, but
apparently Mrs. Mapes made free with her story.

"They were very close," Miss Palin said. "Her daughter
died a year ago, but Mrs. Mapes still wears black." She
shook her head sadly. "Poor thing. I have never seen
anyone so dedicated to mourning."

Lady Griselda nodded. "She never takes off that veil."

"And she takes her meals in her chamber," Miss Palin
added. "It is so sad."

Both ladies wore expressions of genuine sympathy,
and suddenly I felt terribly guilty. They were such honorable, worthy souls, and here I was deceiving them. The
certainty that I would never see them again after this miserable adventure was finished was bad enough, but then

I realized that they'd all be left thinking I was a thief and it hit me like a bolt of lightning; my heart was stricken.

Thieves! I'd spent my entire adult life loathing them, blaming them. The monsters who robbed The Maiden that day took more than a few candlesticks and a till. They stole my life. They stole my parents and my innocence and my youth. I became an adult that day, responsible for The Maiden and for Uncle, for my servants and for the welfare of all of Lower Ridington, for the village depended upon the traffic that stopped at The Maiden.

I was saved from such maudlin thoughts by the return of Mrs. Mapes. Though I could not see her face very well, I knew she was smiling, for I heard it in her voice as she said, "Did I miss anything?"

"Not a thing, my dear," Miss Palin answered, as though they'd been bosom friends for years instead of having just met two days before, "but methinks that if you were but a moment later, you would have missed some fireworks. Here comes Lord Turnbull."

I looked, and sure enough, there was Pos approaching with an alarming purpose in his step. I cringed. *What now?*

"Steady, now," Miss Palin murmured. "Steady!"

"He is only a man," Lady Griselda added. "And you are a woman—a lovely woman. You have the power, not he."

"Am I that obvious?" I hissed.

"Yes!" all three said in unison, and they laughed.

I saw nothing humorous about it.

Completing his circumnavigation of the dance floor, Pos stopped in front of our group and gave a low bow. "Ladies," he said with a nod. "I hope you will not mind if I steal my lovely wife away from you. I have been away from her for an eternity. At least twenty minutes."

The ladies all tittered.

Traitors.

Pos offered me his arm, and I had no choice but to accept. Moving out onto the floor, we joined the set that was forming and, as we were the last couple forming the two long lines of ladies and gentlemen, we found ourselves standing out after the very first set of figures.

"People are remarking that we aren't acting like a married couple should," he said loud enough for me to hear. "I suppose they did not see us on the terrace the other night." He leaned close. "Or in bed this morning," he whispered into my ear, sending a shiver down my spine and raising gooseflesh.

I didn't trust myself to respond. What could I say? *Yes, Mr. Jones, I was quite the wanton trollop this morning, entwined with a naked man on the bed for an hour and pretending to be asleep so I could enjoy it as long as possible!* Uh . . . no. But, then again, I didn't have to *say* it. The gooseflesh on my arm raised by his whisper in my ear did the trick to a nicety. He hadn't missed it, drat him. Reaching out to stroke my incriminatingly bumpy arm, his eyes glinted with a knowing passion. "You were beautiful this morning. You are beautiful now."

That was all it took. Right there, on the Earl of Maddermark's pink marble ballroom floor, I melted into a puddle of sickeningly feminine vulnerability.

I couldn't help it. No woman could have. His voice was soft and deep, his eyes warm and alive. I could *feel* that he meant it. Truly I could! He thought I was beautiful! And I couldn't help *feeling* beautiful.

In all lives there come a few, perfect moments where the entire world is arranged just for them, where everything and everyone are poised for their delight, their purpose, their contentment, and the moments are bliss. They sustain us when the rest of our lives are not proceeding according to plan. They buoy us with the hope of achieving such perfection again and making it last. They are fleeting. Tantalizing. Wonderful.

But I knew in my heart that this moment would be my last. I would never recapture this feeling. How could I? I was swathed in silk, illumined in the perfumed light of a thousand beeswax candles, bathed in swirling orchestra music, adorned with jewels, and encased in fine, white kid at hands and feet, while in a few days I would be back at The Dancing Maiden, serving ale and cleaning tables.

I wouldn't even have Pos's visits to look forward to. I was going to stop him from stealing the sapphire—I already had that day, I was certain, for I'd had either him or the sapphire in my line of view all day long—and I wondered if he would ever speak to me again after this.

I was lying when I said I'd help him steal the gem.

I knew he'd be angry, and truth to tell, it felt wrong, somehow, but he'd forced my hand. There was nothing else I could do. Stealing was wrong, and that was that.

I had to save him from himself!

Our pause in the dance was almost over, and as we prepared to rejoin the line of dancers, Pos bent down and stole a kiss, pressing his lips against mine in a warm buss that felt tender—but I knew better.

"Shielding us from suspicion?" I said, unable to help my wooden tone of voice.

"No. That hadn't crossed my mind. I simply wanted to kiss you, my lady fair."

With that, he swirled me into the parallel lines of dancers. As we wove and dipped through the figures of the intricate dance, he never took his eyes from mine. He wore a soft smile, and each time we came together and touched, it was like the earth was blossoming into springtime.

I couldn't feel more elegant and beautiful. Everything was soft or fragrant, shiny or dulcet. The music propelled the dancers through the figures like a warm, soothing breeze propels leaves across water. It was like a dream.

But it was a dream from which I knew I would soon awaken.

It was going to be difficult to return to my everyday existence, to leave all of this luxury behind. I'd known intellectually how my betters lived, but not having experienced it for myself, I hadn't realized how wonderful it all was, how it felt. Smooth cotton sheets with maids to turn them down at night. Sumptuous meals served on silver and china that I didn't have to cook or clear or wash. Manicured lawns and, inside, vases with flowers of every color tumbling out of them. A doctor on call, water pumped into the house. Hot baths whenever one wished. Perfume flagons. Silver mirrors. Automaton birds that danced and chirruped the hour.

The list was endless. And now that I'd had a taste of it, I didn't want to give it all up.

The dance ended all too soon, and Posthumous escorted me to the perimeter of the floor. "Would you like some lemonade?" he asked.

"Thank you," I said, not really wanting any. What I wanted was for Pos to kiss me once more. Hell, what I wanted was for him to carry me up to our bedchamber and kiss me a hundred times! "Lemonade would be lovely," I said.

"You have only to command, and I will follow," he said with a grin and a bow and moved off toward the refreshments table.

But I wasn't alone for long. Uncle trotted over within seconds, positioned himself stiffly in front of me, and gave a swift bow, his ridiculous purple turban falling off his head and landing in his outstretched hands—hands that, I realized, had already been in place before that turban had started to fall. I narrowed my eyes and peered inside the turban. To my horror, I saw at least a dozen pilfered trinkets there: a quizzing glass, a snuffbox, a few loose coins.

"Aren't they lovely?" he crowed, staring at them lovingly.

"Uncle!" I hissed, trying to shield his turban from view of the other guests. "To whom do these belong?"

"Why, the guests."

"Did you take them all tonight?"

"Yes. Quite a feat. Was almost caught by that crabby termagant over there."

"How do you propose I shall return it all?" I said irritably.

"I do not. I am afraid I do not remember who I took them from. Except for this . . . " He gave the turban a little shake, and out rolled a sparkly something.

"Oh Uncle," I breathed. "Not the sapphire!" My head whipped over to the dais upon which the sapphire had been displayed, only to find that it still was!

Sure enough, the sapphire was still there, resting on its velvet pillow. I looked back in the turban.

"Is this the real one?"

"Of course! The Blackbird doesn't settle for fakes."

"Where did you get it?" I answered that question myself. "Posthumous!" Uncle must have taken it from Posthumous's pocket!

Which meant Posthumous Jones had stolen the gem in front of everyone!

I had to switch the one on display with the one in his turban. Why did he have to borrow that!

Turning Uncle away from the guests, I directed him out onto the balcony where I stuffed the items into my reticule.

I needed to create a diversion. A big diversion. Fortunately, I knew someone who would happily provide it.

"Uncle . . ."

"Say no more!" Uncle put up his hands, as though reading my mind. "Indeed I shall make a distraction!"

He had read my mind! Walking away from me, he made straight for Constance and moments later Constance said, her voice carrying, "I am overwarm! Mr. Bird, I need lemonade!"

"Yes!" He ran to the punch bowl. "There are no cups!" he cried. And with that, he pulled off his turban and used that instead, scooping up a large quantity of lemonade.

By this time they had gathered quite an audience, but not every eye was upon them. Not yet.

Next, Constance slumped onto the floor with her hand

on her forehead. Uncle dashed back, looked at her, shrugged, then took a swig from the turban. "Good lemonade!"

The entire company howled with laughter, and I switched the jewels while somebody gave Constance a vinaigrette.

Everything went as planned. Perfect.

CHAPTER SEVENTEEN

We pardon to the extent that we love.
> —Francois, Duc de la Rochefoucauld

I held out my hand to him, the glinting gem resting in my palm. Would he understand? He had to.

"I couldn't let you do it, Pos. I couldn't let you remain a thief."

He picked up the sapphire from my palm and tilted the blue crystal back and forth in the firelight. "This is the fake! You switched them back!"

I opened my mouth to explain, but he spoke before I could utter a single syllable.

"Thank you."

My mouth dropped open, and I gaped at him. "What?"

He smiled and ran a tender finger down my cheek. "You haven't written your letter to the earl yet, have you?"

"No." I shook my head. "I thought you would . . . that you might . . ."

"You are giving me one more chance to be good?"

I nodded. "You are good!"

"I am not that good, but . . . oh, dearest Apple! Knowing what I now know about you, how could I allow you to become a thief?"

He moved in a step and my heart pattered in my chest. "I could, however, let you love a thief, could I not?"

He lowered his head. His lips touched mine and heat pulsed through my body as he tasted me. I couldn't think. "I do not understand."

Pos raised his head. "Am I not clear in my intentions, Apple?" He let his fingertips flow freely down the outside of my gown, grazing my breast.

I gasped. "The sapphire?"

"Sapphires are not as alluring as apples, my love."

His hands moved over my gown, but I didn't step away or utter a protest. I couldn't. I wanted him to touch me. "Pos . . ."

He buried his hand between my breasts, his kisses touching me where no one else ever had. I couldn't stop him. I didn't want to.

My body fairly hummed as he explored it.

"You blush becomingly. Just like an apple, and I want to take a bite."

He grinned at me, and I smiled. "You are a rake, Pos."

"That's why you adore me. That is why you must have me in your arms." His eyes turned dark and he held out his hand to me. "Come, Apple, my love. This time, we won't be interrupted." He led me across the room to the bed. The rather large bed.

I went. He wasn't going to steal the gem. He wasn't a thief. Not really. Not anymore. He had changed.

"Now, about that ravishing . . ."

"I take it we won't miss each other in the night this time?"

He smiled. "Not tonight. Not ever, perhaps."

He settled me onto the feather mattress, his gaze tender. Suddenly, shyness overcame me. As if he could sense my feelings he held my chin, forcing me to meet his gaze. "Are you afraid?"

I tilted my chin. "Of course not. We have kissed before.

And, if there is a little more," I said shyly, "well, I am an innkeeper. I know the ways of men and women."

"Do you really?" With a small movement, his hand tweaked one nipple, and my treacherous body responded with a gasp and an arching that I had as little control of as I had of the rise and fall of the sun.

"I thought you seemed rather new to the game, Apple. Have you ever felt like this before?"

His hand ran down my leg, then up under my skirt. "Pos!" My body was no longer my own. "I do not know what I am feeling!"

"I do." He sat up and looked at me, up and down, sending glittering prickles skittering here and there. "You are beautiful, my Apple." His voice had gone husky. He shirked out of his coat and waistcoat, and as he pulled off his shirt, I closed my eyes. I dared not look.

Laughter echoed through the room. "Why won't you see me, my love?"

"I don't know."

His took my hand. "You cannot be shy! Not my Apple. Who is this woman in my bed?" He chuckled, and that gave me courage, somehow. My eyelashes flitted open.

His chest was sprinkled with hair! Curly hair, all shiny in the candlelight.

"Touch me," he said, and I did. He folded his fingers with mine. I couldn't tell where my hand began or his ended.

"We were meant to be together."

"I know, Pos. I want to be with you."

He smiled. "You will do anything for me, will you not, my sweet Apple?"

His fingertips tickled my skin. My body was no longer my own, and it nodded and murmured, "I am yours."

His smile turned devilish. "You trust me?"

"Yes. Of course."

Why was he dallying about? I was certain there was more to this ravishment business than just talk!

"Let me have you the way I've dreamt, little Apple. At my mercy."

Taking a velvet cord—the bell rope!—he twisted the fabric around my wrists. He pulled them above my head and wrapped the cord around the brass headboard.

My heart thudded in my chest. "What are you doing?"

"I want you to be mine, my love. I want you to be tied to me for a lifetime as you're tied now to the bed, for the rest of our lives."

"What are you saying?"

"Will you marry me, Apple? Will you be my wife?"

I couldn't look away from him. His body pressed against mine, chest to chest, thigh to thigh.

"Will you be mine, Apple?"

His breathing had quickened. Strain decorated his face.

I didn't care if my arms were bound. My heart was already tied to him. "I will."

He groaned and touched me . . . and I was carried away on a journey of emotions, of feelings, of inexplicable connection. Presently, all conscious thought drained away from me, and I knew why that soft expression graced so many women's faces when they spoke of the bedchamber. I could feel only him, the man I would marry. We were bound; we were one; we always would be . . .

. . . She was mine. She'd given me the gift of her innocence, and I couldn't prevent the awe from touching my heart. Normally, after I'd brought pleasure to a woman, I would joke, we would laugh, we would complete the passionate promise. We would make love. My Apple was different.

She was true, good, and deserved to see her wedding night a virgin. And yet I couldn't stop myself from running the back of my hand down the smooth and milky texture of her arm. Her skin so smooth, her heart so pure.

I had offered her my hand in marriage. My heart clenched. She had accepted me. I couldn't fathom why. I didn't deserve her. I'd done too much, seen too much.

She stirred against me, and my body responded despite my best intentions. A lifetime would never be enough time to be near her.

Her deep brown eyes opened and drew me closer as a smile danced in their depths. "I didn't know . . ." she whispered.

I kissed her forehead as my heart swelled with devotion. She was an amazing woman! "I know. Can I tell you something you can never share with a living soul?"

Her tongue moistened her lips and I groaned. She could tempt me with more guile than a Siren and she was totally unaware of her allure. "I didn't know either, Apple."

She shook her head. "Isn't it always like that?"

I smiled at the innocence of her question. "No, my love. What we have is special. We have only just begun. Our wedding night will offer you even more."

Her eyes widened. "More?" She pulled at the cords around her wrists. "I want to touch you."

I kissed her, tasted her sweet breath mingling with mine. "I think I like you this way." Her body lay before me, flushed and ripe. She wanted me as much as I wanted her.

She smiled broadly. "You just don't want me to get away."

A stabbing hot poker skewered my heart at the words. Too many memories. "It's happened before."

I burrowed my face into her neck, searching for a warmth from the chill cloaking my body. She nuzzled my neck. "Tell me, Pos. Who left you?"

I lifted my head and met her gaze. Her face, soft with compassion, commanded honesty. "You must know all of me, Apple. As I know you. There can be no secrets between us."

She swallowed and then grinned. "But in the daylight, there is so *much* of you. I can feel you. I can see you."

I chuckled. I truly did adore her.

I retrieved the sapphire and lay it between her breasts. "This is why I'm here, Apple. The sapphire brought me here. But its wealth goes far beyond money. I am not here for riches. I am here for my mother."

Silent expectation reigned on her face. She didn't quiz me, just waited, silent and patient.

"The sapphire belonged to my mother, Apple."

She gasped. "Your mother? But I thought . . . "

"I know what you assumed. You were partly right."

I fingered the blue gem, memories cloaking me in comfort. "See how it shines, how it sparkles. The authentic sapphire has depths I can't describe. I remember staring at it, playing with it as she cuddled me. I know every angle, every contour of the sapphire. The sapphire and my mother are linked."

"Which is how you made the fake so real."

The certainty in her voice made me smile. "No . . . even I couldn't have done that. A fake arrived with the letter I received." Retrieving the worn foolscap from my valise, I read the letter aloud and then looked into her eyes. "I didn't need this job. I haven't stolen anything for years. I have invested, Apple, and done well."

"You are rich."

"I would have been. But I give all of my profits away."

"You are trying to atone for your sins."

I did not deny it. "Until I received this letter I didn't know how thankful I was to be a thief. If being a thief brings my mother back to me . . ."

Apple twined her legs in mine as I tried to move away. She'd trapped me with her heart and her body. I recognized I'd lost my independence. I'd gained more than I lost, however.

"What happened to her Pos? How did she lose the sapphire? How did you lose her?"

I sighed. "The worst day of my life. I had just turned eight. A man came and stole the gem from her. She cried. I remember her tears. Her face was covered with them the last time I ever saw her. She went after the thief and never came back."

She studied my face, and this time it was I who couldn't meet my Apple's gaze. She saw too much. I flopped back on the pillow.

"Just eight!" she whispered.

"Eight." The word croaked from me and Apple gave a small gasp of dismay.

"You were a child."

"I was old enough to survive. I waited for her. I waited right on that street corner for three whole days, until hunger drove me into the streets. No one knew where she was. The room we shared was empty and cold. And soon it belonged to someone else. Before long, I was starving, faint from hunger. And I joined a gang of street thieves to survive."

"You could have been hurt, killed."

I shook my head and gave a grim smile. "No. I had a mission. I would become the most accomplished thief to ever roam the countryside. Then, one day when I found the sapphire, I would steal it back. For her."

"That day has come." He bowed his head. "My mother was a good person, kind, educated, and soft-spoken. She was the daughter of minor gentry, gently brought up."

"That explains it! Your voice and manners always said 'gentleman' even when your clothing did not. She taught you how to speak and behave!"

"She taught me more than that. She taught me stealing is wrong, and I was able to bury that fact, until you. I am ashamed. She would have been ashamed at what I have become." I pulled away from her. What was I thinking? I was unworthy of loving her.

"Untie me, Posthumous," Leah whispered. "Set me free."

Her words squeezed my heart in pain.

I unknotted the fabric from the bed, though the rope hung from my Apple's wrists. She cupped my face in her hands. "You had no choice. She would understand. She would have forgiven you. She understood that sometimes actions are necessary. She worked in a brothel to survive."

"She was poor. Her parents had died, and she was alone. But she knew it was wrong. That's how she finally came to London. To look for work. She was educated, good with a needle. Constance often gave her extra work, to help her. We visited the brothel, but Mama preferred her mending to the other life."

"That is how the ladies of The Birdhouse know you!"

I nodded. "I do not remember visiting The Birdhouse in those days, but when I . . . visited it later, Constance recognized me immediately. She said I looked much like my mother. And I never did sample her wares."

"Oh!"

"Did you think I had?"

"At first." She toyed with the velvet on her wrist. "Your life was hard, wasn't it?"

"We were poor, but safe—or so we thought. If Mama had stayed at the brothel . . . maybe . . ."

"What about the sapphire? Surely it was worth a fortune."

"She would not sell it. I thought nothing of it at the time. I knew she treasured it above all things, save me. I realize now that she was probably murdered while attempting to retrieve it. "

A tear fell from her eye down her cheek. I wiped it away.

"Don't cry for me, Apple." I gave her a crooked smile. "My life turned out for the right. I met you. I have found my path."

"But you have lost your mother. Oh, Pos! Did you think stealing the sapphire would help you find her?"

"When I was little, I thought that maybe Mama would come if only I had the sapphire. And that's why I am a thief."

"*Were* a thief."

"I'm a bloody brilliant thief, Apple." I pushed away the

shadows. She needed to understand, but I'd made my peace.

She pulled me down to her and held my body next to hers. "You are a man of honor, Posthumous Jones. No matter what name you use. I am sorry I doubted you." She held her arms out to me.

I couldn't resist her; I let my body ease onto hers and ground against her, kissing her, loving her. Her warmth enfolded me and I was home—for the first time since I was eight years old . . .

. . . He was a hero. My hero. My match. My mate. And soon he would be my husband. I laughed with joy.

"Mr. Jones. Thank you."

He kissed my mouth, my cheek, my forehead. "Thank you, soon-to-be Mrs. Jones."

I ran my hand along his chest. "I should have known when I saw you in the Blackthorn village that you were more than you seemed. It's no surprise the people in every village are always so glad to see you. You are their guardian angel. You make their lives easier."

He flushed. "I do what I can, but the truth is I deserve no praise. My motives were more selfish than not."

"Why do you continue to see yourself as unworthy, Pos?"

"I traveled far and wide looking for the sapphire, making amends along the way, but I am no angel, Apple." I shook my head and threw her a wry smile. "If I were divine, I would have known how close I was to the answer. I have traveled through Maddermark village a hundred times. The sapphire was so close, and I never knew it."

"Do you think your mother is here?" I whispered.

His voice broke. "Part of me always wondered if she'd found the sapphire, come back to see I was a thief, and abandoned me for it. She was a virtuous woman, in spite of her circumstances."

I shook my head. "The woman you have described

made her own sacrifices, Pos. She wouldn't have let you go if she'd found you."

"I know that—now. But as a child, I always doubted . . ." He sighed and I held him to me. "She must be dead, Apple. So what am I doing here? Why am I stealing again?"

"You are taking back what rightfully belongs to you, Pos."

"That's the thing, Apple! I am not stealing it for me, but for her."

"And I am going to help you!"

Pushing him to his back I . . . I ravished him back! My breathing was short, my body purring when we finally pulled apart.

"You are an amazing woman, my love," he said.

A quick glance at the sun coming through the window and he jumped out of the bed. I felt cold as his body left me. "We must make our appearance acceptable."

With experience I didn't ask myself about too carefully, he helped me reassemble my garments until I looked more presentable.

"Sit here, my dear. Let me slip on your shoes."

I lowered myself to the chair and Pos let his fingers caress my leg behind my knee as he encased my foot in my slipper.

"Pos!"

He grinned. "I don't want you to forget what we shared, my love. Let me remind you again." Open-mouthed, I stared at Pos as he used the velvet cord which had brought us so much pleasure once to tie me again, this time to the chair.

"What are you doing?" I asked, though I knew very well what he was doing, and I was filled with a quivering delight.

He finished tying me and stood, then he pulled a clean handkerchief from his pocket and tied the linen around my mouth. He had gagged me, the rake!

"I can't let you go with me, Apple," he said sorrowfully. "I won't allow you to risk it."

"Mmm?" I cried, my voice muffled.

"I am truly sorry, my love. I have tied you for your own good."

He completed dressing and I watched, stunned.

He was going to leave me there! Everything he'd said was a lie! He was going for the sapphire! Would he leave me there? Tied? Would I ever see him again?

He turned to me and shook his head, as if he could read my mind. "Don't let the doubts take over, Apple. I see the terror in your eyes. I understand it." He leaned down to kiss my cheek. "I do love you. And I will return."

I groaned, pulling at my bonds, trying to scream at him, but no sound but a strange grunting came from behind the gag. He leaned down in front of me. "What we have is real, Apple. I am going to do the right thing. Listen carefully," he said, kissing me on my forehead, stilling me. "I didn't steal the sapphire at the ball, as you thought I did. I still have a fake in my pocket. Which means, my love, there are *three* sapphires. And another thief out there trying to take the real one!

"I am going to go find the real sapphire and take it back, one way or the other. This other thief, whoever he is, isn't going to like that, and thieves—as you know all too well!—can be nasty. If you're untied, you will follow me, love, I know it. And you could get into trouble. I can't put you in any danger. I won't."

I bowed my head, an ache throbbing in my temple.

"I will save the sapphire, and it will be the last thing I'll ever steal," he said. "I promise."

He closed the door on me and left me alone in the room, the tousled bed proof of our activities. Could I believe him? I struggled against my bonds, but only a few seconds passed before the door opened to me and my eyes widened.

Uncle John followed Pos into the room. "Leah? What happened? Who did this?"

I rocked the chair back and forth and Uncle strode toward me.

Pos stopped him. "John! Stop. There's another thief here, trying to steal the sapphire. I tied her to keep her out of trouble while I go look for it. You stand guard. She won't be able to wander into harm's reach if she's restrained. Otherwise, you know she'll talk you into letting her go."

A gleam twinkled in my Uncle's eye, and I knew I was lost and stuck in this chair for the foreseeable future.

Pos pocketed a few items and kissed my forehead once more. "Trust me." His eyes begged me, but I raised my chin. How could I trust him fully, when he obviously didn't trust me enough to not help him? On the other hand, if he'd let me go, nothing would have kept me in this room.

He tilted his head once more as if he could hear my thoughts. "I do trust you, Apple, but I know you too well." His smile dropped. "I refuse to put you at risk."

"What if you're caught?" Uncle John asked. "Who will take care of Leah then?"

"I won't be. You know that better than anyone." He pulled out a peacock feather from his pocket.

The Peacock. I was in love with the Peacock. The rake. The ruffian. The thief.

John laughed. "Good hunting, my feathered friend." From his own pocket, he drew forth a blackbird feather and held it up smugly. "I would trust no other to pull off the job."

"You are the Blackbird?" Pos cried.

"None other!"

They both laughed, those two men whom I trusted more than any.

Pos slid out the door, and Uncle turned back to me.

"He's doing what he thinks is best." He pulled the gag from my mouth.

"We cannot let him face this alone."

"He must," John said. "He can't be distracted by his love for you. He and I both know you're safer in this bedchamber."

I opened my mouth to speak, but a warning pierced me from Uncle's eyes. "I will gag you, Leah, if you don't behave. Posthumous needs to have his wits about him. There's still a player out there whose identity remains a mystery. I know these people, my dear. They are a nasty lot. Most think nothing of slitting throats."

"You didn't. Did you?"

"Of course not! I am the Blackbird," he said, as though that explained everything.

"Mr. Jones could be in danger. What if something happens to him? What if he's caught taking the gem? What if the thief stabs him or shoots him or—"

"You must trust him, Leah. You must give him your faith."

I didn't remember allowing sleep to overcome me, but a gentle kiss on my forehead woke me. "Apple, wake up."

I twisted in the chair and as I stared upon his countenance, I smiled. "Pos, you're safe."

He untied the velvet holding me to the chair and I couldn't resist throwing my arms around his neck before I stepped back, hands on my hips. "If you ever tie me up again, I won't be responsible for my actions."

He lifted an eyebrow. "I thought you rather enjoyed it, my dear."

Heat rose up in my cheeks and a small cough from behind Pos turned into a chuckle. Constance shut the door behind her and Uncle, dressed in his bizarre costume.

"Good Lord, Uncle, what are you wearing?"

"We don't have time for this, Posthumous."

The smile left Pos's face. "You're right. We have a problem, Apple." He pulled a gem from his pocket. "The sapphire I stole is a fake."

"That's impossible. I put it there myself."

"Someone already has the real one. This isn't going to work. Someone knows."

"How is that possible?"

"I don't know and we have no time to discover the reason. We have to leave. You're in danger. Come."

"What about my clothes?"

"We're leaving them, Apple. We're all pretending to go for a drive and we're not coming back."

"I'll be relieved to leave this behind, Pos. We can start our life together."

I glanced out the window, one last look before we left. A carriage clattered down the courtyard. "Someone's coming. Perhaps we can take their carriage," I said.

Pos joined me at the window and looked down below us in time to see a young lady and gentleman getting out, a crest on the side of their black lacquered coach.

Pos frowned. "It cannot be!"

I met his stunned gaze.

"The viscount has come to England early."

CHAPTER EIGHTEEN

Out of the frying pan, into the fire!
—Old English Proverb

"Who is it, *mon cher*?" Constance asked.

"Stay here!" I hissed and bolted for the door. Slipping soundlessly down the hall, I ducked into an empty bedchamber closer to the carriage, dashed to the window, and peered at the crest. Swearing, I ran back down the hall, no longer bothering to be quiet.

"The Viscount and Viscountess Turnbull are arrived. The real ones. To the back stairs, quickly! We've no time to waste! Out!"

I'd been wrong! I didn't know how it happened, but somewhere I had miscalculated, placing Constance, Apple, and Mr. Bird in terrible danger. I urged the women none too gently through the doorway, but they both looked wildly around and cried out in unison:

"Where is Uncle?" "Where is John?"

I looked around. The old man was gone.

"Did you see him leave?" I demanded.

Both ladies shook their heads vigorously. "No!"

"Mr. Bird!" I called. "John!" But there was no answer. He'd simply vanished.

"Go!" I ordered. "Give me five minutes—no more!—
and then leave whether we are there or not! Stay off the
North Road and make for The Birdhouse."

"The North Road would be faster," Constance warned.

"Wait a minute!" Apple cried. "We aren't going anywhere without you and Uncle!"

I ignored her and addressed Constance. "The side
roads will take you twice as long, but they will be safer. Do
not hurry. It will be best if you do not appear to be running from anyone. Now, move! With any luck, John and
I will be waiting for you at home when you arrive."

"Come, *cherie*," Constance told Apple. "We must do as
Pos says."

"The hell we must! I'm not going anywhere until—"

"Can you knock a man unconscious with your fist?" Constance asked her.

"No."

"Pos can. We will only slow him down. Now, run!"

But she didn't move. She was paralyzed with fear.

Giving her hands a squeeze, I looked deeply into her
eyes. "I will bring him home, Leah. I promise."

They ran.

"Man!" Amy said. "This is intense!"

"Shhh!!!" every other young woman hissed.

"Here," Erma said, opening a new journal for the first
time. "This belonged to Mr. Bird. Read starting"—she
touched the page—"right here."

Stephanie took the book eagerly and read. "'No more
of this foolishness,' the earl said, shaking . . ."

. . . shaking his fist in anger and pacing across the
ballroom floor in agitated slashes. "I have already exposed myself to enough ridicule. Admit it, John. Your plan
has failed!"

"No, no!" I cried. "You must do as I have suggested, William. Please. Summon everyone to the ballroom. No exceptions. Everyone must be brought here. Now!"

"What madness is this?"

"It is the only way you will have your wish, I tell you."

"My wishes are dead. They died a long time ago."

"I don't believe that."

The earl shook his head in disgust. "She is not here! If she were, the sapphire would be gone. I will dispose of it forthwith. I will sell it to the highest bidder. Or give it away! I do not care. Would you like to have it?" He laughed mirthlessly. "It means nothing to me now."

"You know I do not crave riches. I never have."

"I know." The earl sighed and raked his hand through his dark, curly hair. "That," he said tiredly, "is precisely the reason I chose you to take the gem from her in the first place. I could trust you not to take it for yourself. I trusted you for more than that."

"You mislaid that trust."

"No, old man. I know you have tried your best. Ah . . . what a pair we are, eh? A poor thief who has all he wants and a rich earl who has nothing."

"I do not have everything. I want the same as you; a woman I cannot have."

The earl sat on the edge of the dais. "What is it you want me to do?"

"Please, my lord. Make haste. Summon them all—the guests, the servants, everyone—as I have asked."

"I will as long as you drop that 'my lord' claptrap. We have been friends too long for that, John."

"Quite right, your lordship. Now move your noble rump!" I motioned to two footmen. "You and you! Come here."

"Yes sir?"

"Each of you take one of my arms and stand next to me, as though I am your prisoner. And hold on tight, no matter what. Things might get a little rough!"

"Beg pardon, sir?" One footman scratched his head.

The senior of the pair looked to the earl for confirmation. "My lord?"

The earl gazed skyward and shook his head. "Just do whatever he says." And then he moved away, muttering, "There is not enough brandy in the world. . . ."

"William!" I called after him.

"What?" he said irritably.

"Send footmen to find the Viscount and Viscountess Turnbull and Lady Turnbull's companion!"

John Bird—the Blackbird! The Peacock's fiercest rival!—was nowhere to be found. Not in the parlors nor the kitchens nor the garrets. I searched, literally, high and low. I sought out every cranny and nook, investigated every closet and commode larger than a turnip.

I sneaked around like a blasted cat burglar, ducking around corners, crawling behind armchairs, sniffing around settees, and rolling beneath feather mattresses like a hound on the hunt, remaining undiscovered by the sniveling Portman Lowell, who, even now, I could heard downstairs calling for my blood.

All an all, I was acting very unlike a viscount!

I turned another corner, and yet another. The passageways streaked past. I heard the footman shouting below and a scramble of boots on hardwood floors and stone passages. There was no time to lose!

I redoubled my efforts and charged into a room I hadn't yet searched. The bed hadn't been made or else had been recently mussed, and perfume wafted like a love potion, but the room was empty of body and soul. Hearing a familiar voice issue from the open window, I poked my head through and peered below. A glimpse of dark hair, a white petticoat, and the rush of tiny feet encased in satin pumps—Apple! And Constance close behind her. And then they were gone.

Ducking back inside, I peered downstairs, where men in black and women in silks—the guests!—scurried about like a swarm of insects, all mixed in with servants of every description.

Why?

Someone out of view shouted, "Have you seen him?"

"Who?" was the prompt answer, this from a scullery maid pressed into extra duty.

"The viscount."

"I'm looking for him myself!"

I tore my gaze away. If I couldn't find John Bird, I wouldn't be joining Apple and Constance in that blasted coach!

Someone had left a goblet on the bedside table. Brandy. I took a gulp and said a silent thank you to the unknown philanthropist who left the unfinished nightcap behind—a woman, judging by the frilly undergarments left on the divan and the heady perfume still lingering in the air. Upending the entire contents down my throat, I dropped the glass on the bed and charged away, courage coursing through my veins and my head abuzz.

I had no idea where I was going. My footfalls resounded against the walls, sprang up and down the staircases, reverberated as the mere thought of Apple echoed inside my heart. The very sound of her name—Leah—repeated like a prayer inside my head, rang like a church bell. Her mouth, her skin, her eyes. I wondered briefly if Apple worried about me as much as I worried over her. But I shouldn't have. She loved me, by God, though I didn't know why!

What if I couldn't find John Bird? A chill ran through me like an omen. What if time ran out? I'd soon find out . . .

I called for him. "Blackbird!" I cried at the top of my lungs, wishing the sound to conjure him like a ghost from the vapors.

The only place I hadn't searched was the first floor. The

public rooms. I heard people gathering in the hallway, the
ballroom, the parlor, meandering like ants in an anthill,
their insect legs skittering and scratching. Snippets of
voices carried up to me. Their voices echoed, some deep-
throated and furious, others high spirited and incensed.
They were being summoned to the ballroom forthwith.
Commanded! And they didn't know why. The ladies were
particularly virulent and I heard language such as should
not be heard in a drawing room of gentlemanly company.

If I went down there, I would be caught. And so would
he . . .

The hair stood on the back of my neck, and my senses
sharpened. Letting them lead the way, I ran over thresh-
olds, tossed back drapes, and threw aside bed linens. I
heard it then. The pounding of a pair of stiff boots trudg-
ing up the rear staircase.

"Viscount Turnbull! Come out, come out, wherever you
are, for I shall find you, quick as a wink, even if you hide
beneath your lady's skirts!"

Portman Lowell.

I listened and watched, squatting there in the tight
corner, crouched behind a knight's suit of armor riv-
eted securely to its armature, my hand on my boot where
I wore a concealed knife.

He turned and bobbed, and called out my name again
and again, initially as a curse and then as a question.

His footsteps plodded on. He met a servant and
inquired.

"Yes, m'lord," I heard the servant say. Then, "No,
m'lord." His voice receded, calling back, "I shall go for
him and tell him you are waiting."

The first set of footsteps, however, refused to budge,
stuck as if mired in clay, waiting for a telltale sign—a gulp
of trepidation or a cackle of glee.

"Coward," I heard Portman intone. "Coward! Have
you no shame?"

He marched back the way he had come. "You are a blackguard! A thief. A rake."

His footsteps shuffled, scraped, drew nigh.

And I, in my dread, pulled farther back, though I wanted nothing more than to pummel him into the ground.

Suddenly, he pushed into a room across from my hiding spot. "Aha!" he shouted like some mad musketeer and then stilled, disappointment reeking in his voice. Before I knew what was happening, I had left my inadequate hiding place, jumped through the room's open window, and landed on the ledge outside, clinging to the stone for dear life.

On the move once more, Portman progressed, step by deliberate step. He leaped forward, his cane leading the way, and probed behind the velvet curtains, poking and prodding. And then he poked his head out the same window I had just leaped through, twisting his head to and fro and grunting in irritation before marching off, giving up the hunt.

Cautiously I sidestepped along the ledge, a little too cautiously for a grown man. The wind was at my back, gratefully, but the ledge was narrower than the width of a boy's foot, and I clung with all my strength and guile to the stone outcropping, swearing under my breath at the day my path crossed that of Portman Lowell.

Inch by inch, I made steady albeit niggling progress, and as I gained ground, each toehold a torturous progression, wondered how on earth I had flung myself out that damnable window, flew like a bird on wing over the sill and onto the ledge, and there stood, looking down at pavement that, should I fall, surely would have broken my neck in an instant. Such are the miracles of life! But to get back inside—that was a different matter altogether.

I made it, needless to say.

With a final breath, I lowered myself into the room. The ceiling swirled above while below, my heart thudded. I waited a few seconds, no more, trying to catch my breath and realized I heard no more running along the corridors, no more padding along the floorboards, no more shouted names or challenges riding on the wind.

I sat up and, gathering what self-respect a thief, a liar, and a bogus viscount could muster, reeled to my feet. I knew what I had to do. I had little choice. The drama was about to unfold. I might as well step from behind the curtain onto the stage.

It had been more than five minutes. Leah and Constance would be safe by now, on the old carriage road, winging their way back to The Birdhouse. It was the least I could do, to present myself like a man and not a mouse.

I'd searched everywhere for John Bird. The only place he could be was downstairs in one of the public rooms. And that way led certain capture.

Or did it?

With a flounce and a jump, I perched my derriere on the banister and flew down the grand staircase, nary a whisper to be heard—a brilliant maneuver, had I not picked up speed. But, as I neared the bottom, I spun out of control and landed with a marked thump on the floor, same derriere taking a beating.

The sound attracted the attention of a footman, who, spotting me, trotted over. "Your presence is requested, m'lord, in the ballroom."

"Is it?"

"They're all waiting for you."

"It's a sad, sad day when I man cannot act like a boy and not be dressed down for his behavior."

"Yes, sir." His voice was stern but his mouth curled.

I had gained an ally. Even if the silly goose couldn't do a blessed thing for me, at least I had his moral backing.

Like a dandy, with a flourish and sweep of my cape, I entered the ballroom. They had all assembled there, every one. Lords, ladies, and servants alike; cooks with spoons still in hand, grooms with grass covering their boots, scullery maids with coal pans in tow.

The earl and Uncle John were in there too, so much for my scavenger hunt. Clearly, John was not there of his own volition. He was held by two burly stablemen, though that was hardly necessary. What kind of fight could an eighty-year-old man brook?

Also in the room were the real Viscount and Viscountess Turnbull. Given my entrance, I couldn't very well blend in with the others, even though I mightily endeavored to do so.

The earl noticed me at once and cried out. "There! There is Viscount Turnbull!"

I was at the point of placing myself behind a potted plant but sidestepped the philodendron.

I was just about to duck down and make my way out of the ballroom when the real viscount bellowed, "*I* am Viscount Turnbull! And *you* are an impostor! Where is your false viscountess?"

That, as Apple would have said, was that.

I pushed myself to the fore and bowed. The formality took him by surprise. "Are you speaking of the beautiful Leah?"

"If that is her name, I am."

"Well, sir, you are wrong about her. She is honorable and true, even if I, by self-proclamation, am not."

In defense of Portman Lowell, he could not know what a self-effacing prig he was, or how heartless. "I knew the girl to be a trollop," he said, stepping forward. "I knew it as sure as I'm standing here. I've known her for years. And I can tell you, you can dress them up, but you cannot wash away the stain of common blood."

He presumed to continue hurling out accusations, but I curtailed his intent by hurling another item of fiercer measure. My fist.

Striking at once at his jaw and his Adam's apple, my fist connected with a resounding crack of bone and sinew. I felt a deep sense of satisfaction, but my merriment was destined to be short-lived.

I'd bloody well broken my hand!

I nearly passed out. Certain I had broken every bone in my hand, dashing hero that I was or no, I nevertheless hid my agony behind a grimace and bared my teeth. I think I growled—whether from audacity, vertigo, or lunacy, I am unsure—and slumped to my knees. I had every intention to get to my feet and strike him again, but two big men grabbed me from behind and pinioned my arms behind my back.

"Take him away!" cried the earl. "Filthy thief!"

And here I saw my fate rushing before my eyes. Transportation. Chains and filth, bread but once per day, unclean water, and the daily scourges from a cat-o'-nine-tails until I made it to some godforsaken island dead or alive. But it wasn't that which bothered me, but the thought that John, Constance, and Leah would join me.

I'd given up too soon.

All at once, a clattering, crashing sound broke through the bedlam of the ballroom, and Constance and Leah burst through the door, astride two horses and leading two more behind. To me they looked like angels from heaven.

"Posthumous! Uncle!" Leah shouted. "Hurry! Jump on!"

Tearing myself away from my captors, I made a bounding leap and took to saddle.

Mass confusion followed. As if the two women and four geldings were tantamount to the hordes of Asia, everyone ran for their lives, screaming and bleating.

"Uncle! Uncle!" shouted Leah. "Quickly!"

The earl screamed at John. "You? You in league with these rogues! I should never have trusted you! You were only here to steal it! To steal the sapphire from me!"

John only stood there. He made no effort to mount. Instead, inexplicably, he smiled.

As long as I live, I will never forget that.

* * *

Constance and I had not gotten far down the back stair
when a voice scolded us from below. "You'll be wakin' the
dead stompin' around like that." I hesitated and was
bumped from behind by Constance.

"Do not tarry, *mon cher,*" she urged quietly.

We rounded the corner of the stairwell and were met by
the momentarily angry visage of the butler. He was clearly
surprised to find two of the earl's guests hurrying down the
stairs in such a rush, and recovered his composure immediately. "Pray watch your step, my ladies," he muttered,
giving a sidelong glance at the expecting viscountess—
me!—and then allowing himself a disapproving look at my
companion.

"Yes, do take care," Constance echoed, rolling her eyes.
The butler caught her look and gave Constance a quizzical look.

"May I be of assistance, then?" He signaled to a passing maid to approach, and Constance wrapped her arm
lightly about my waist, guiding me toward the door.

"Yes, if you please. The viscountess has been struck by
the vapors, and is in need of a stroll." The butler strode
purposefully to the door and held it open, simultaneously
waving off the maid. "Very good, my lady."

We glided out the door and across the rear portico, and
Constance pretended to assist me down the remaining
stairs for the butler's benefit. "There now, the air is pleasant here. Shall we walk this way?" Constance gestured
toward the livery stable. We strolled arm in arm, chatting
gaily, as the door closed discreetly behind us.

Quickening our pace then, we were soon in view of the
front drive and the elaborate coach of the Viscount Turnbull. There was obviously some confusion afoot; his footmen stood awkwardly by awaiting orders. A Maddermark
footman approached the coach, gesturing with the calling card that the unfortunate viscount's footman had presented, and voices were raised. I could imagine the earl's

butler: "My lord, it appears that we are *doubly* honored to receive you!"

A hysterical giggle rose in me, and I thought for a moment that I might actually take on the vapors.

"Shhhh. Listen," Constance hissed. The voices from the front of the house became louder.

". . . so then, who are the others?"

"Take the viscount's bags inside and locate the other Viscount and Viscountess Turnbull! Quickly!"

We shrank into the hedge shadows and scurried toward the stable. Soon there would be a party looking for Pos—and us!—and the blasted butler had taken notice of us leaving out the back.

"What now?" I asked Constance.

"We shall have to ask to have our carriage readied quickly. Should they ask, we will tell them that we are taking a drive."

We ducked through a parterre to the carriage path and walked swiftly along the far side of a tall hedge. We couldn't be spotted from the house from there, but if riders were to come along, we would be caught. As luck would have it, we were twenty yards from the stable when the Viscount Turnbull's handsome coach came down the path. In a panic, I pressed Constance into the hedge and scrambled in behind her. In doing so, I tore some of that fine silk that my erstwhile husband had purchased for me—and probably left some flesh behind as well.

Constance hit me in the face with an elbow as she pulled twigs from her lovely hair. "Sorry," she muttered. "I know why you pushed me in here, but next time just tell me to hide." She managed a laugh, and I admired her thrice over.

The coach rolled past us as we peered anxiously from the bushes. Constance pursed her lips and appeared to be deep in thought. "I believe we could use that," she observed. "The house staff is probably looking for us at this very moment, and we will likely not have time to have our own carriage readied."

"Stealing a carriage? And horses?"

"Borrowing, my dear. Borrowing!"

Though it seemed like a good opportunity, reaching the stable did not look easy. A groom was visible at the head of the drive, pacing back and forth, and the front of the stable was well lit and visible from the house. We were adequately hidden by the hedge, but we would have to expose our position to move anywhere else.

Looking back at the house, we could see lights aglitter in the upper floors. What was happening inside? They must be searching for the impostors. What would they do to Pos and Uncle if they found them? Worse yet, what would they do if they found Pos *with the sapphire?*

"I cannot leave them here," I moaned.

"I do not want to leave them either," Constance said. "But men are put on earth to protect women, and you have seen that Posthumous is very capable. They can use their resources to best advantage if we remain at a safe distance, as they told us."

She was right, of course. By following their instructions we were more likely to be safe, and they would be able to concentrate on their own safety. But Constance and I might escape and not know for days and days whether our men were out of harm's way!

"The two men we love most in the world are inside that house. How can we save ourselves and leave them here?" I breathed deeply and evenly, staring back at the lamps moving in the house, and finally turned and looked at Constance. We held each other's gaze for a moment, and then she broke off, turning her own attention to the house.

Shaking her head, she gave a grim little smile. No words passed between us, but we were of a single mind. There was no decision to be made—we simply would not leave. Not without Pos and Uncle. Taking my hand, she dragged me out of the bushes, branches catching our hair, scratching our faces, and tearing our gowns. We ran headlong along the path, heedless, hoping that the groom at the drive entrance was more interested in his end of the drive than ours.

The viscount's footmen seemed eager to deliver their charges and be gone. A pair of plane trees flanked the entrance, and Constance and I dashed for one of them, since the outlying lanterns were burning bright. We needn't have been quite so cautious, for it was brighter still in the stable itself, and I doubt the grooms could have seen more than ten feet up the drive. But at that point we were more concerned about being seen from the house.

The two grooms admired the coach and its team with great enthusiasm. The first one rubbed his hands across the rich wood surface and fingered the gilded crest on the door.

"A lovely piece o' work," he crooned. "Haven't seen it's like before."

The other groom nodded appreciatively, giving his attention to the matched grays. "You should look at the horses then," he replied, clearly impressed.

"What are we going to do?" I whispered, knowing that if we were close enough to hear them, they were close enough to hear us.

Constance looked me up and down and lifted a skeptical eyebrow. *You look a sight,* she seemed to say. It was true, and she looked no better; our hairstyles had come loose, our faces were scratched and our dresses were dirty and torn. Had we looked like a viscountess and her dresser, perhaps we could haughtily demand a carriage. But at this moment, no one would believe we had a right to be there.

As we watched, the grooms pulled the luxurious traveling coach into the stable and began to unharness the horses. "Whatever it is," Constance said, "we have to do it quickly."

I watched while a strap was loosened. "Follow me," I told Constance as I left the hedge.

"Help, help!" I screamed. From behind me, I heard Constance shouting too.

"What is it?" the groom began, then he looked at us as if wondering what two such disreputable women were doing on the estate.

"Men." I sobbed and pointed toward the drive. "My friends and I." I took a deep breath. "My friends and I were walking down the driveway to greet the new arrival, and two or three men jumped out."

Constance sobbed. "The dastards. They attacked us." She put her hand to her throat. "They took our jewelry and ran off." She paused dramatically and pointed. "Go after them."

"Don't know if we should," one of the grooms said. "We've got this carriage to take care of."

I sobbed again, dabbing at my eyes. Indeed, the tears came easily because I had just wiped tree sap into the right one.

"Go after them," Constance repeated, gesturing with even more emotion.

I shivered as I realized what a terrible lie we had told and that I wasn't going to stop lying. Pos was right. Things aren't always black and white. I had to lie to save him. Real anger boiled out of me, and I turned to Constance.

"Instep will be pleased to hear how his stalwart defends the honor of his guests!" Stamping a foot for emphasis, I whirled about and stalked off in the direction of the house.

"You would allow those ruffians to harm a delicate woman?" Constance sniffled piteously. She hurried to catch me and took my hand. We turned toward him together, one of us angry as a nest of hornets and the other helpless and beseeching.

They didn't know us from Adam, but you could have read the grooms' faces as you would a book. Not "the earl" or "Earl of Instep," but simply "Instep." A woman who referred to the earl so casually was likely well placed, and the grooms took another appraising look at us.

"At your service, ma'am," the first said, and he lit out down the road. He got a dozen steps away and called over his shoulder, "Follow me!" whereupon his companion looked helplessly at the team, then at us, then at his disappearing comrade.

"Well, follow him!" Constance bellowed, and the young groom reddened and tore off down the drive.

We watched them vanish beyond the lanterns, and I stood there shaking.

"We'd best hurry," Constance said. "We don't have very much time."

I hurried to the strap that I'd seen the groom loosen a few moments ago. Long ago I had learned to hitch up any vehicle that came to the inn, and tightening the strap was little problem. I was not looking forward to driving however, and turned about to see whether Constance was in the coach.

To my surprise, she was already mounted in the driver's box with the reins in hand. "Hurry!" she urged.

I don't know which surprised me more: her familiarity with a carriage team or the agility with which she mounted the seat. I began to follow, but she waved me off.

"Get in the coach! Now!"

I got inside.

Pos had told us they would meet us in "five minutes— no more" and it had certainly been longer than that by half. That meant that he and Uncle John were in trouble. Constance shook the whip, cracked the reins, and drove the team out the other side of the stable. The hooves and coach wheels made a great deal of noise within the shelter of the stable, and at once I heard the shouts of first one groom and then the other from somewhere behind us. The team pulled through to the other side of the stable and Constance expertly guided them through the come-around. By the time we reached the drive, we could see the grooms running toward us, shouting. Constance cracked the whip again and the team obediently and instantly leaped forward. The grooms rightly judged that they couldn't stop two tons of horseflesh, and leaped aside into the same thorny hedge that we'd just escaped, poor dears. The coach passed them by, increasing in speed with every turn of a wheel.

My heart was pounding in my ears and I barely heard Constance call out to me. "Leah! Keep a close watch for the men!" I did as she bade, but there was no sign of Pos and Uncle John. Indeed, all was quiet outside, meaning that the search for them had likely concluded and they were trapped inside.

The footman had noticed our commotion, and for some reason was running in our direction. Instead of closing the gate to trap a wayward coach, the footman was attempting to intercept us with his bare hands. *Men!*

We burst through the gate, slowing enough to make the turn onto the road.

I craned my head out the window, calling to Constance. "They will mount after us presently! We'll have to abandon the coach!"

"Yes, and quickly! They will overtake us in short order! How long will it take you to unhitch the team?"

"Five minutes," I said, not truly believing it.

"You shall have three if we are lucky!" I heard the crack of a whip, and the coach surged again. The earl's manor was on a hill, and the only way out was down. At least the night was fully moonlit.

But where to hide a coach? It simply could not be done, not here on the hill, and not below in the village. How to make time?

The hill flattened out and Constance slowed the team to cross the river into the village. The stone bridge leading into Maddermark village crossed at a point where the embankment was steep. It was perhaps possible to ford the river here, but one would be better off crossing

farther upstream or downstream. I leapt to my feet, leaning out the window. "Stop! Constance, stop! Stop on the
bridge!"

The horses slowed on command, and the coach
eased onto the narrow bridge, easily blocking traffic
in either direction. "Pull the team forward onto the
bank," I commanded.

Constance did so, and set the brake.

Where did she learn that? I mused. *I must ask after we're
transported!*

I opened the coach door and it swung wide, revealing
a misty ten foot drop to the rocky stream below. There was
hardly any room to pass between the wall and the coach,
so I let myself out carefully and tip-toed forward on the
wall, steadying myself first on the coach's gilded panel,
then by holding fast to the team harness. The horses
nickered with satisfaction; they'd had a good run and were
glad to be past the bridge.

Constance awaited me, having dismounted and
squeezed past on the far side. She was full of surprises. I
wondered if there were anything she couldn't do. I fer-
vently hoped she would not disappoint me now.

"Help me unharness this team!" I cried. She went to
work alongside me and, while she lacked my strength and
my expertise in the stable, Constance was a quick learner.

We led the team away one by one until the four grays
were detached. Looking up the hill toward Instep's estate,
I imagined I could see a cloud of dust in the moonlight,
coming directly toward us. The chase was on, and I hoped
for a miracle.

"Let us ride, *chérie!*" Constance tugged on the reins,
leading the horses away toward a tree that had been
overtaken by old age and now lay nearly prone. I hadn't
thought that far ahead: Constance would surely know how
to ride, but could she ride bareback? She certainly
couldn't ride astride! Would we be able to mount the giant
beasts at all, and would they allow themselves to be taken?

I despaired, even as I heard the distant thunder of hooves coming down the hill.

"Hold these three and steady my mount," Constance shouted, taking command.

I did as she asked as she carefully crawled up the tree on all fours, her gown hitched up in front of her most immodestly. Having gained some height on the horse, she stood up on the tree with an awkward sway, took her gown up with one hand and a fistful of the horse's mane in the other, and swung her leg over the horse's back and pulled herself up.

It was the most coarse, undignified, unladylike, and magnificent effort I'd ever seen, and I laughed despite myself.

Then it was my turn. I shall spare you the awful detail, but suffice to say that I took three attempts to mount, and that I was for the first time glad to have the extra padding behind me that the Lord saw fit to provide.

"Ride down into the village!" Constance cried, nodding downstream. "Our pursuers can likely see us now. We'll double back when we can."

"Constance, we have to go back for Pos and Uncle John. Is there a place we can cross the river upstream?"

"Lud, I hope so!"

We flew. The groomsmen were right; the horses, even though carriage steeds, were thankfully well behaved and responsive to our crude touch. The Viscount Turnbull spares no expense in his stable, it would seem. We lost sight of the bridge and wondered how long it might take for the party to cross after us.

"Turn off here." Constance pointed up a small side path, partially gravelled, leading to an orchard of pears. We filed up singly with Constance leading, and rode carefully off the beaten path. Hopefully the gravel and the night would obscure our trail. Sure, and we're whistling past the graveyard.

Into the orchard we went, where the horses left a track

a blind man could follow come morning. At least we
were out of sight of the river; we turned back upstream.
We planned to ride as far as possible in this direction until
we were forced back to the road. Perhaps we would miss
our pursuers, perhaps not. At the moment, we didn't
know where they were, and they had lost sight of us.
Hopefully they would continue on the last path they'd
seen us take, into the village, and search for us there.

The insects were fearsome in the grove, and they seemed
to be attracted to the blasted lemonade that soaked Constance's bodice. I slapped myself and used language that
Constance would not have allowed in The Birdhouse—nor
I in The Dancing Maiden! She said nothing to me, but I
imagined I saw her smiling once or twice in the moonlight.

The orchard was no more than an acre or two, and it
gave way to a more-or-less open field that was obscured
from the highway by a slight roll in the earth. We passed
a stone boat and made a note to watch for rocks in the
darkness. It didn't occur to us that we were trespassing.
The earl owns most of the surrounding countryside, and
any villager that happened upon us would recognize us
as a patron of the earl and worthy of their respect.

Past the field, through another small orchard, and
then we entered a wooded area—dangerous to traverse
during the daytime, let alone night. It was time to make
our way back to the road, and so we threaded in and out
of the woods until we reached the river. Constance and
I had come out a half-mile upstream of the bridge, and
the river was shallower and more accessible here. It was
also rocky and the horses' feet would be unsteady. It
would have been wise for us to dismount, but there was
no obvious way for us to remount there with no obliging
trees upon which to stand.

"Onward! No time to dilly-dally!" I shouted.

"Yes, we are exposed here."

"We will have to return to the estate the same way we
came down."

Constance shrugged. "They will dispatch another party for us."

"Not until dawn. And it has only been a half-hour since we left."

"It feels like a week."

"Mm!"

We presently rejoined the road leading up to the earl's estate. A quick flick of the reins, and the horses broke into a trot, happy to be moving again at a more respectable pace. But our hearts fell the closer we came to the estate, for we had no idea what we were to do. How to rescue our men? We could only perch somewhere outside the gate, watching for any slim opportunity to come along.

So that's precisely what we did.

We led the horses off the road and tethered them to a shrub. Then we walked boldly up the road within view of the gate—which was still open for some reason—and the front portico. Then we disappeared into the brush and watched for our men.

Botheration! Poor Constance! The mosquitoes on the hill liked lemonade, too.

Mrs. Mapes turned to me. "Apart
Bird stole the sapphire from me—

CHAPTER NINETEEN

*Being deeply loved by someone gives you strength, while
loving someone deeply gives you courage.*

—Lao Tzu

"Oh, Pos!" Leah cried. "I am sorry. I tried—"

"Shh . . ." I held my finger to my mouth.

The earl turned to Mr. Bird. "Uncle?" he exclaimed.
"Uncle? You are in league with these people! You never
had any intention of helping me lure her here! You were
only trying to get your filthy hands on my sapphire!"

"Helping him?" I demanded.

The earl turned to me. "As though you do not know!
That won't do you any good, thief!"

Apple cried, "He is not a thief! He was only taking what
was rightfully his!"

"Tell your lies to the judge! Take them all away!"

"No!" a woman shouted, and something shot across the
wide, marble floor, skittering to a glittering, bumping stop
at the earl's feet. Mrs. Mapes stepped forward. "There is
your blasted sapphire! They didn't steal it. No one did."
And then she lifted her hands and threw down her heavy
veil.

The earl gasped. Beside him, John Bird smiled, and

Mrs. Mapes turned to me. "Apart from the hour Mr. Bird stole the sapphire from me—the day you were lost, my son!—I have had the gem in my possession these twenty-eight years!"

CHAPTER TWENTY

A man would always wish to give a woman a better home than the one he takes her from; and he who can do it, where there is no doubt of her regard, must, I think, be the happiest of mortals.

—Jane Austen

We were married that Christmas in a double ceremony with Posthumous and Leah. The earl and his countess—Ruth, Pos's mother!—served as witnesses. The little chapel closest to The Birdhouse was filled with green and hothouse flowers. Constance wore white, as she deserved to, and her eyes were shining and proud. She was so beautiful I wept.

As Vicar Sweet and the village children were to perform their pageant that night, the place was filled to the rafters with wise men, shepherds, sheep, and angels—not to mention a lovely bevy of birds, a flotilla of proud seamstresses, and a few secretive souls who nodded their final, silent salutes to me or to the Peacock and then simply faded away.

Neither of us will ever leave a feather behind again.

Just before the ceremony, Ruth presented Leah with a wedding present, her sapphire on its golden chain. Setting it round the girl's neck, the countess kissed her cheek. "A symbol of perfect love," she said.

The earl kissed Leah's other cheek and shook first Pos's hand and then mine. "We none of us need such a symbol. We all have the real thing in our grasp!" Finally, he bent over Constance's hand. "Thank you, ma'am. For everything."

Constance gave a gracious nod, and the ceremony began.

Constance here.

There are some parts missing to my husband's story. He says he is too busy spoiling his grand-nephews, and too much time has now passed to think he will ever finish this memoir, so I shall record the missing events myself.

Miss Ruth Jones was the daughter of minor gentry, who lost her parents at the age of sixteen and lived by her wits until I took her in. Her first gentleman caller at The Bird-house was the earl. She was not beautiful, but she had gentle sweetness about her, piercing blue eyes, and a merry laugh that made every heart glad that heard it. The young earl fell in love with her immediately, and though he paid me a large sum to keep Ruth only to him, he would not touch her or behave in any way other than a gentleman might with a lady in public. When she reached the age of consent, he proposed marriage, and in a flash of joyful insanity, she agreed. They ran away to Gretna Green, where he gifted her with an extravagant wedding present—the sapphire, which was worth as much as one of his minor estates.

For three days, they tarried.

For the earl, those days were the happiest of his life. But then she left him, taking the gem with her. The sale of a sapphire so large and perfect would have allowed her to live in comfort all her life, and he concluded that was all she had wanted from him and that she did not love him.

He was wrong, of course.

Ruth had realized Society would never forgive him for marrying so far below his station. Any children she could bear him, the offspring of an imprudent lord and a common whore, would never be fully accepted. Guilt crashed down upon her. She'd been mad, foolish, naïve, and utterly selfish to agree to a Gretna wedding.

And so she ran. She knew the marriage would not be legal in England unless they both signed their parish register and showed the paper the parson in Gretna Green had given to them. If she never signed, if she simply disappeared, she reasoned, he would be free to go on with his life as though she had never existed.

Knowing he would come looking for her, she abandoned her old life, abruptly and completely severing all ties with The Birdhouse, and she moved to London, finding work there as a seamstress.

Soon, she realized she was increasing.

She struggled with the dilemma before her. Keep the child a secret or go to the earl. In the end, she kept her secret, naming the boy Posthumous and telling everyone his father had died right after they were wed. It wasn't a good decision, I think, but she has regretted it and suffered for it enough. And the two of them led a happy, if frugal, life together. They loved each other dearly, and Posthumous was a good boy, sturdy and intelligent. Ruth wanted to send him to school but couldn't afford it, and she often wrestled with the idea of applying to the earl for aid once Posthumous was old enough.

It was a choice she never had to make.

A few days after Posthumous's eighth birthday, a man stole her sapphire. She realized he'd taken it just in time and ran after him, leaving Posthumous waiting on a street corner, her golden medallion in his hand.

The thief, of course, was my husband. His real name was John Black—the Blackbird, as he was known in certain circles. But he was no ordinary thief. He was a master of his craft, and he was also, incongruously though it may seem to those who do not know him, a good man.

The earl had been sold a glass copy of the sapphire along with the real gem at the time he acquired it. Such

copies are often made to foil would-be thieves, but the Blackbird had sometimes made use of them to help him steal!
He had the copy along with him that day, should the occasion arise to use it, and it did—but not in the way he'd
expected.

Realizing the sapphire and its golden chain had been
taken from around her neck, Ruth followed John and,
against all odds, caught up to him, clever girl!

I do not know everything that was said between them
that day, but I know what was not said. Ruth neither admitted she loved the earl nor said anything about Posthumous. And yet, though John had no way of guessing
about the boy, it wasn't difficult to see that Ruth was still
deeply in love with the earl, for she obviously led a
meager existence and yet had not sold the stone.

Moved, John gave her back the real stone and went on
his way.

And then, in her rush to get back to her son, Ruth was
run down by a mail coach that thundered down upon her.
She nearly died, and it was a week before she was even
awake. She sent someone to look for him, but by that time
it was too late. He had disappeared.

She stayed in London, never giving up hope of finding
him, but her little boy was lost to her, and she was lost to
me.

And then one day, her son, a boy of fifteen or so,
walked into The Birdhouse, wearing her medallion. I
knew who he was as soon as I saw him. I gave him her old
room, the Peacock room, and over the next twelve years,
it was the closest thing to home he had.

But the story does not end there.

On the way back to the earl's estate, the glass copy still
in his possession and the real gem still around Ruth's
neck, John had two more glass copies made. He passed
one of them off as the real thing to the earl, who locked
the painful object in a box and never looked at it until
the house party, almost twenty years later. The earl hadn't

wanted the sapphire, he'd wanted Ruth. By sending John to steal the gem, the earl had hoped to draw her to him.

He wanted to look into her eyes and see for himself that there truly was no love there. Only then could he free himself, he believed. Only then could he fall out of love.

But it wasn't to be. She never came.

That was John's fault, and he was never easy about it. "It is queer," he would say. "So much suffering might have been avoided if only I'd not interfered and left events to unfold as they were meant to."

He knew the earl well and me, of course, and he had seen Ruth the once. Then, nigh on two years ago, he chanced to glimpse a feather and realized "Mr. Morgan" was really none other than the Peacock, his greatest rival.

John began studying him, learning about him, and saw that he was not only a good thief but also a good man, and then, finally, one evening at The Dancing Maiden, John saw Pos toying with his mother's golden medallion.

Suddenly, all of the puzzle pieces fell into place and John realized he had a unique opportunity to set things right. The earl and his lady could be reunited with each other and with their son. The Peacock could realize his birthright. Leah could be settled with a good husband.

And John could at last marry his only love—me, I am proud to say.

But first, four stubborn, strong-willed people would have to clear away the claptrap that crowded their brains.

The earl was sure Ruth had never loved him.

Ruth was sure Society would never accept their love.

Leah was rigid and controlled, and she recognized only absolutes.

Posthumous was convinced he was unworthy.

And the only way John could think of helping was to bring everyone together, to mix them up like bicarbonate of soda and vinegar and watch them explode!

It worked.

EPILOGUE

If we are incapable of finding peace in ourselves, it is pointless to search elsewhere.
— Francois, Duc De La Rochefoucauld

"It is ironic," I said, lazily stroking Apple's temple, "that when your name was Grey, you could only see black and white, while now that you see the world in shades of gray, you find that your name is really Leah Black!"

"Not anymore," she said, snuggling next to me. "I am now Lady Mrs. Posthumous Leah Black Grey Stone Morgan Jones, the Viscountess Woodsmere!"

"Nee Turnbull, do not forget."

She laughed. "I think there can be no fear of that!"

I was happy.

I was reunited with my mother, who was deleriously in love with my father, a good man I was coming to care for a great deal. They had signed the parish register, making their marriage valid, which meant I was a viscount and Apple, as my wife, a viscountess.

Meanwhile, Constance and John were living their own happily-ever-after. Apple had convinced me I'd atoned enough—or, rather, that I'd never had any need to atone—

but we'd decided to keep giving back anyway, and the best way to do that, the most fitting way, was to see that The Birdhouse continued its mission. We endowed it with a large contribution so it was self-sustaining without being a place of . . . business. It would still be a school for young ladies who had lost their way, as it had always been, but it would no longer be a brothel.

Apple gave Constance the real sapphire for that purpose, but it turned out that The Birdhouse didn't need it. John had his own fortune tucked away, and Constance keeps the sapphire as a sort of insurance policy, just in case.

Now, Apple, my mother, and Constance each wear a copy of the sapphire about their necks. Apple never takes hers off. Even in bed.

"When do you think the house will be finished?" she asked.

We were having a large cottage built near The Birdhouse to live in while visiting John and Constance, which we planned to do often.

"About the time our child is born, I should think."

"Pos! I am not with child! Am I?"

"Perhaps not, but you will be."

"Mmm . . ."—she smiled—"I must learn to tie better knots." She nibbled my arm, her eyes glinting mischievously in the candlelight. She was a surprisingly passionate and playful woman, yet I managed to make her blush often enough. We were well-matched.

I reached to toy with the bauble dangling at her neck. "You look wonderful wearing only a fake sapphire and a smile. Who would have thought that the responsible, efficient, orderly Leah Grey would be such a siren?"

"Nothing is what it appears to be on the surface," she said, "and sometimes, what appears to be flawed is the most valuable. This"—she covered my hand with hers, enclosing the sapphire in my fingers—"is a perfect gem."

"Me or that sapphire?"

"Both. Now, hand me that rope."

* * *

"Time for bed!" Erma sang out. "It is late, and I have been a pushover to allow you to stay up so long on a school night."

Most of the present-day ladies of The Birdhouse attended university. The folded up their laptops and their books and went to their rooms, calling their goodnights and sighing at the happy ending.

Erma smiled and, gathering the journals, opened the wooden box once more and replaced the volumes. But, before she locked it and set it back on the mantel, she paused.

Reaching in, she pulled forth a sapphire—*the* sapphire.

It had been restrung with pearls, and it glowed in her hand just as the story glowed in her heart. She was the eighth keeper of The Birdhouse. And, just like Constance, so long ago, she was leaving in the morning to live her own happily-ever-after.

Her replacement was arriving tomorrow.

She sighed, smiled, and locked the box. "And they lived happily ever after!" she said.

More Regency Romance
From Zebra